W9-BLI-050

SLITHER NO MORE

Fargo went down the hallway to the back door. He opened it slightly and peeked out the crack. He saw a couple of privies and a rain barrel. There was no sign of Snake.

That didn't mean he wasn't there. Fargo opened the door a little wider, and Snake popped up from behind the rain barrel. He held the shotgun tight against his good shoulder with both hands.

Fargo slammed the door as Snake fired. The buckshot rattled off the walls of the house, and Fargo flung the door open. Snake had dropped back down behind the barrel.

Fargo shot into the barrel near the bottom. There was water in it, and it drained out the hole.

"The barrel won't do you much good when the water's gone, Snake," Fargo said.

Snake jumped up, the shotgun pointed at Fargo's mid-section. This time Fargo didn't give Snake a chance to pull the trigger. He shot him in the bridge of the nose.

Snake's head exploded in a haze of blood and brain matter. . . .

THE TRAILSMAN

#307

MONTANA
MARAUDERS

by

Jon Sharpe

A SIGNET BOOK

SIGNET
Published by New American Library, a division of
Penguin Group (USA) Inc., 375 Hudson Street,
New York, New York 10014, USA
Penguin Group (Canada), 90 Eglinton Avenue East, Suite 700, Toronto,
Ontario M4P 2Y3, Canada (a division of Pearson Penguin Canada Inc.)
Penguin Books Ltd., 80 Strand, London WC2R 0RL, England
Penguin Ireland, 25 St. Stephen's Green, Dublin 2,
Ireland (a division of Penguin Books Ltd.)
Penguin Group (Australia), 250 Camberwell Road, Camberwell, Victoria 3124,
Australia (a division of Pearson Australia Group Pty. Ltd.)
Penguin Books India Pvt. Ltd., 11 Community Centre, Panchsheel Park,
New Delhi - 110 017, India
Penguin Group (NZ), 67 Apollo Drive, Mairangi Bay,
Auckland 1311, New Zealand (a division of Pearson New Zealand Ltd.)
Penguin Books (South Africa) (Pty.) Ltd., 24 Sturdee Avenue,
Rosebank, Johannesburg 2196, South Africa

Penguin Books Ltd., Registered Offices:
80 Strand, London WC2R 0RL, England

First published by Signet, an imprint of New American Library,
a division of Penguin Group (USA) Inc.

First Printing, May 2007
10 9 8 7 6 5 4 3 2 1

The first chapter of this book previously appeared in *Nebraska Night Riders*,
the three hundred sixth volume in this series.

Copyright © Penguin Group (USA) Inc., 2007
All rights reserved

 REGISTERED TRADEMARK—MARCA REGISTRADA

Printed in the United States of America

Without limiting the rights under copyright reserved above, no part of this
publication may be reproduced, stored in or introduced into a retrieval sys-
tem, or transmitted, in any form, or by any means (electronic, mechanical,
photocopying, recording, or otherwise), without the prior written permission
of both the copyright owner and the above publisher of this book.

PUBLISHER'S NOTE
This is a work of fiction. Names, characters, places, and incidents either are
the product of the author's imagination or are used fictitiously, and any resem-
blance to actual persons, living or dead, business establishments, events, or
locales is entirely coincidental.
   The publisher does not have any control over and does not assume any
responsibility for author or third-party Web sites or their content.

If you purchased this book without a cover you should be aware that this
book is stolen property. It was reported as "unsold and destroyed" to the
publisher and neither the author nor the publisher has received any payment
for this "stripped book."

The scanning, uploading, and distribution of this book via the Internet or via
any other means without the permission of the publisher is illegal and punish-
able by law. Please purchase only authorized electronic editions, and do not
participate in or encourage electronic piracy of copyrighted materials. Your
support of the author's rights is appreciated.

The Trailsman

Beginnings . . . they bend the tree and they mark the man. Skye Fargo was born when he was eighteen. Terror was his midwife, vengeance his first cry. Killing spawned Skye Fargo, ruthless, cold-blooded murder. Out of the acrid smoke of gunpowder still hanging in the air, he rose, cried out a promise never forgotten.

The Trailsman they began to call him all across the West: searcher, scout, hunter, the man who could see where others only looked, his skills for hire but not his soul, the man who lived each day to the fullest, yet trailed each tomorrow. Skye Fargo, the Trailsman, the seeker who could take the wildness of a land and the wanting of a woman and make them his own.

Montana Territory, 1860—Nick Williams once saved Skye Fargo's life. Now he's been murdered, and the Trailsman is going to do something about it. Skye Fargo has faced bad odds before, but this time he has to take on a whole town.

1

Skye Fargo never felt comfortable on a steamboat. It wasn't that he'd never traveled on one. He'd once gone down the Mississippi from St. Louis to New Orleans on a gambling boat just to take part in a high-stakes card game.

But the experience hadn't been a pleasant one. He felt cramped and closed in on a steamboat. He was called the Trailsman, and he was more at home on the back of a horse, somewhere out on the prairie or in the mountains, guiding some pilgrims down a well-known trail that they couldn't travel on their own, or making a trail where there had been none before.

In a way that was what he was doing now, if you could call the Missouri River a trail. He was taking Mrs. Jane Cudahy and her daughter, Marian, to join Mr. George Cudahy in Fort Benton, Montana. Cudahy had been there for months. It was his idea that opening a store there would be a way to get even richer than he already was.

Gold had been found in Virginia City, and Cudahy believed that the miners on the way there would, for the most part, be coming through Fort Benton. They'd need supplies, and he was going to sell them. At a profit—a big profit. The store was open, it was showing a profit, and Cudahy wanted his wife and daughter to join him. He also wanted someone trustworthy to see that they got there safely. Skye Fargo had taken the job, but the Cudahys didn't want to travel the overland route. They preferred more comfortable surroundings than a wagon, so Fargo found himself on a steamboat.

He stood on the second deck under the nearly cloudless blue sky and looked down at the murky water of the Missouri as it flowed by. He wouldn't ordinarily have taken the job of delivering the two women, but after he'd met them, he changed his mind.

Or maybe Marian Cudahy had changed it for him. He wasn't quite sure. At any rate, he was on the *Chippewa*, and they were almost at their destination. It had been an interesting trip, in more ways than one.

When Fargo had traveled the Mississippi down to New Orleans, he'd been on a boat with a pilot who'd studied the river for years. The man knew every snag, sandbar, and sunken boat along the way. But since no one had ever taken a steamboat all the way to Fort Benton on the Missouri River, the hazards weren't as well-known. There were no sunken steamboats, but sunken logs were ready to tear the bottom out of the boat, and sandbars could strand the ship for days. Nobody knew for sure where they were. They knew the signs to look for, and that was all.

So far there hadn't been any major problems. They'd scraped by a sandbar, but it hadn't slowed them down much. They'd had a couple of rainstorms, but those had been no trouble at all. The boat was almost to Fort Benton, and Fargo could relax. It had been an easy trip.

Not that it had all been pleasant. There were a number of unsavory characters aboard, like the two men called Possum and Snake. They didn't look like miners to Fargo. They looked like a couple of hardcases. He thought they were probably back-shooting varmints, and he'd had trouble with them almost from the beginning of the trip. They hadn't waited long before they'd tried to press their attentions on Marian.

They'd backed off when Fargo confronted them, but he'd kept an eye on them ever since. They didn't seem like the kind to give up without a fight, though they'd stayed out of his way for the rest of the trip.

Mrs. Cudahy came out of her cabin and joined Fargo at the rail. She was a stout woman in her late forties, and her iron gray hair was drawn into a tight bun. She carried a parasol to protect herself from the sun.

"I want to thank you, Mr. Fargo," she said, "for tak-

ing such good care of me and Marian. I'm going to rec-
ommend to my husband that he pay you a bonus."

Fargo grinned inwardly. If Mrs. Cudahy knew just how
well her daughter had been taken care of, she wouldn't
have been recommending a bonus. She'd have been de-
manding that Fargo be keelhauled.

"I appreciate that, ma'am," he said.

Marian joined them. Like her mother, she carried a
parasol, but she also wore a wide hat tied under her chin
with a red ribbon. She looked as demure as a schoolgirl.
Her clear skin and open, wide-eyed gaze added to the
impression of innocence that she gave. Her wide red
mouth and soft curves gave the lie to that impression,
Fargo thought, but her mother probably didn't notice
those things.

"I think Mr. Fargo's bonus should be quite generous,"
she said. "I'm sure no one else Father might have hired
could have cared for us the way he did."

She stood on the side of Fargo opposite her mother
and gave him a little nudge with her elbow as she spoke.

"No need for a bonus," Fargo said. "I've had the company of you two lovely ladies, and that's enough of a
bonus for anybody."

He meant that sincerely, though again not in the way
Mrs. Cudahy might have understood it.

"You're very kind," Mrs. Cudahy said. "When will we
arrive at Fort Benton?"

"We should get there in about an hour," Fargo said.

"Is it as lawless and wild as they say?" Marian asked.

Fort Benton was not a military operation. It had
started out as a trading post, and it might have remained
nothing more than that if not for the discovery of gold.
Now a sizable town was growing up around the fort.

"It's not exactly lawless," Fargo said. "I haven't been
there in a while, but I've heard they've hired a town
marshal. There's likely to be more trouble in Virginia
City, where the miners are going."

"Trouble can be exciting," Marian said, giving Fargo
another nudge.

"Maybe. More dangerous than exciting, I'd say."

"What about the place they call Sundown?" Mrs. Cudahy said.

"Never been there," Fargo said.

Sundown was an outlaw town, filled with saloons and populated mainly by prostitutes and desperadoes. It was located to the east of Fort Benton, out in the Missouri Breaks, a wild and desolate area that for years had been a hideout for men who had plenty of reasons to avoid the law, men like Possum and Snake, Fargo thought.

"It's not a place anybody would want to go to," he said. "Not even for excitement."

"You are a spoilsport, Mr. Fargo," Marian said. "You will visit us in Fort Benton, won't you?"

She didn't nudge him this time, but the way she said *will* let Fargo know what she meant. She'd been the one paying visits on the boat. Every night, after her mother was asleep, Marian would leave their cabin and come to Fargo's. She hadn't been coming for conversation.

"I don't plan to stick around for long," Fargo said.

"But you must have dinner with us, at least," Mrs. Cudahy said. "I'm sure George has built a comfortable house for us, and we'd like for you to see it."

Fargo said he'd visit if things worked out. He didn't plan to stay around Fort Benton any longer than he had to. When the *Chippewa* made its return trip to St. Louis, he was going to be on board.

The docking of the steamboat was a big event in Fort Benton. Most of the town's prominent citizens were there, and there was even a brass band. Not a very good one, Fargo thought, but it was loud, and that was all anybody cared about.

He helped Mrs. Cudahy and Marian through the crush of passengers crowding down the gangplank. There were prospectors and sharpers, businessmen and hardcases. Fargo was careful to avoid Snake and Possum.

After they'd debarked, Fargo located Mr. Cudahy, a thin man with a pinched face and glasses that perched on his long nose. Fargo stood aside to let him greet his wife and daughter.

"Come by my store later this afternoon, Mr. Fargo," Cudahy said after the brief reunion was over. "We can settle up then if that's all right."

Fargo noticed that there was no mention of a bonus or

4

a visit to the new house, but he didn't complain. He said he'd find the store later, and the Cudahys set off to see to their baggage, except for Marian, who lingered behind.

"You will come and visit, won't you? Promise?"

Fargo thought he might get a bonus, after all. "You mean come through the front door and into the parlor?" Fargo asked. "Or through the bedroom window?"

Marian tapped him on the shoulder with the tip of her folded parasol and gave him an impish grin.

"You are an evil man, Mr. Fargo."

As she spoke, Fargo looked past her and saw Possum and Snake walk by. They studiously ignored Fargo, which bothered him more than if they'd spoken to him.

Marian turned her head to see what Fargo was looking at. She gave a slight shudder.

"I didn't really mean that you were evil," she said. "But those two are."

"You don't have to worry about them," Fargo said. "We won't be seeing them again."

"I hope you're right," she said.

Fargo hoped so, too. Men like those had a bad habit of turning up when you least expected them.

Fargo looked around the unprepossessing town. The streets were rutted and muddy, the buildings raw and unpainted. Fargo could smell the freshly cut wood. He'd seen many places like it, and many that were worse, but to someone from St. Louis it must have looked like the tail end of civilization.

Marian looked around as well.

"It's not so bad, is it?" she said, trying to sound hopeful, but Fargo could tell she thought it was pretty bad, and maybe worse than bad.

"You'll get used to it after a while," he said.

She looked doubtful. "I think I should have stayed in St. Louis."

"Your mother and father need you here."

"They don't need me. They want me where they can keep an eye on me."

"And you can't very well blame them for that," Fargo said. "Can you?"

Marian touched his shoulder with the tip of the parasol again.

"I've changed my mind," she said. "You are an evil man. Promise you'll visit me tonight."

"If I can find the house."

Marian grinned. "You'll find it, Fargo. I don't think anything could keep you away."

Fargo returned the grin. "You're right about that," he said.

2

Cudahy had already paid for Fargo's return trip, and Fargo planned to spend part of the night in his room on the *Chippewa*. The boat would be loaded by noon of the next day and would start back down the river in the afternoon.

After collecting at the store, Fargo had asked Cudahy casually about his house and learned its location. Fargo fully intended to pay Marian a visit sometime long after night had fallen. If things worked out, he and Marian would have one last chance for a sporting encounter.

Until then, Fargo needed a place to kill some time, a place where he could get a drink and a meal. Cudahy recommended a place called the Big Strike.

"In spite of its gaudy name," Cudahy told him, "it's not a bad place to eat. The portions are generous, and the prices are fair. Fair for a place like this, I mean."

Towns that were on their way to growing from a handful of people to a population of over ten thousand in a matter of months weren't known for their appeal to those of a frugal nature. Prices for everything were likely to be outrageous. Fargo was familiar with that fact, but having just been paid, he thought he could handle the expense of one meal and a few drinks.

He left Cudahy's store and made his way down the crowded boardwalk for a couple of blocks, turned to his left, and found himself only a few steps away from the Big Strike, which hardly resembled its name. It was a small café behind a new false front that looked as if a strong wind would rip it away. But Fargo could smell

7

food cooking, and the smell was a good one. He went inside.

There were six or eight tables, only a couple of which were occupied. It was a little early for supper, Fargo supposed, but there hadn't been a meal on the boat that day, and he was ready for food.

He had venison roast that wasn't too tough, potatoes, and coffee, which was the best thing he was served. He decided that Cudahy wasn't much of a judge of food.

After he finished his meal, he drank a third cup of coffee and left. He'd find a drink somewhere else.

It turned out to be harder than he thought it would. There weren't nearly as many saloons in Fort Benton as he'd thought there would be.

"Drinks are scarce around here because of Sundown," said an old-timer Fargo stopped to ask where the nearest saloon could be found.

"What's Sundown got to do with anything?" Fargo asked.

"That's Whit Anders' town." The man gave Fargo a quizzical look from beneath his bushy brows. "You ever hear of him?"

"I've heard a thing or two."

"I can tell you plenty, but talkin' makes me mighty thirsty."

"Take me where I can get a drink, and I'll buy one for you," Fargo said.

The old-timer, who said his name was Buck Terrell, led Fargo to a place called the Silver Slipper. As they walked through the town, Fargo thought he saw Possum slink into an alley, but when they got there, no one was in sight.

Fargo shrugged it off. Fort Benton was still a small town. Possum was as likely as Fargo to be looking for a place to eat or a place to drink.

"Here it is," Buck said. "The Silver Slipper."

It was nothing more than a shack on the outskirts of the town. As far as Fargo could tell, there was no silver around, and there were for sure no slippers. The place was small, crowded, and smoky. No women could be seen.

"Anders has got most of the women, too," Buck said.

He was short, bewhiskered, and wrinkled. His old black hat looked as if a buffalo had chewed on it. "If you know what I mean."

"You were going to tell me about it."

"Better get us a drink first. I'll have a whiskey."

Fargo bought a bottle at the bar and took it and a couple of fly-specked glasses to the table Buck had claimed. He sat down and poured the first drinks. Buck knocked his back and wiped the back of his hand across his whiskery mouth.

"Ah, that hit the spot. Fill 'er up again."

"Tell me about Sundown," Fargo said, moving the bottle out of Buck's reach.

"You're a hard man, Fargo." Buck eyed the bottle hopefully, but Fargo didn't relent. "All right, it's like this. Whit Anders has robbed and kilt more than his share of folks over the years, and he's spent a lot of time hidin' out in the Missouri Breaks. Some other desperadoes were doin' the same, and before you know it, there was a sort of a town out there. Not exactly a law-abidin' one, either."

He pushed his glass forward, and Fargo poured him a drink. When Buck had swallowed it, he continued.

"Don't need much law in a place like that. Women, whiskey, maybe somethin' to eat now and then—that's what you need. Anders liked the setup, and he got the idea that he'd make himself the law there, except, like I said, there ain't much law. Whatever Anders says, goes. He runs the place, and he makes the people who come there pay him if they stay. They have to pay for the hotels and liquor and women, too. And speakin' of liquor . . ."

Fargo gave Buck another shot of whiskey, which Buck downed immediately.

"Thanks. Well, another thing Anders likes is havin' it so that the people comin' into Fort Benton have to go to Sundown if they want to get 'em a woman, or do any gamblin', or have a good drink. Speakin' of which . . ."

He pushed the glass forward again. Fargo took a swallow of his own drink before he poured for Buck.

"I see what you mean about a good drink," Fargo said. "This isn't one."

"Best you can get here." Buck picked up his glass and tapped it against the table. "I ain't complainin'."

Fargo poured, and Buck went on with his story.

"Folks around here don't like Sundown, not one little bit. They don't like havin' a town full of outlaws that close by, and they've tried to close it down. Ain't had no luck, though. Who's gonna go up against Anders and a town full of killers? I guess Stuver's crazy enough to do it, but he can't get hardly anybody to go with him."

"Who's Stuver?"

"He's the town marshal here in Fort Benton. Rex Stuver. Not much of a lawman, but he can keep order. Hell, it's easy for him. Ever'body's scared he'll shoot 'em if they don't do what he says."

"He sounds as bad as Anders."

"Not quite. The difference is that Stuver's a fella who goes by the laws on the books. People can understand that. It's people like Anders and that bunch in Sundown they're afraid of."

"But they won't go in and shut the place down."

"Didn't I just say they're afraid? There's no profit in goin' after Anders. He'd kill you slow and painful if you crossed him, and he'd enjoy it, too. That's the way they do things in that town of his."

Thinking about Sundown reminded Fargo of Possum and Snake. He wondered if they might have been headed in that direction. They seemed like the kind of men who'd be right at home in Sundown.

Buck asked for another drink and got it. The level in the bottle was going down fast, and Fargo had hardly drunk anything at all. That was fine. The liquor was bad, and anyway, he wanted to be sober for his visit later that evening.

"Worst thing of all," Buck said, wiping his mouth, "is that Anders comes to town now and then to raise hell. That's why Stuver was hired, to tell you the truth. Not to keep things in line here but to keep folks safe from Anders. When he comes to town, he takes what he wants. Don't matter to him what anybody says."

"You mean he steals?"

"That's right. Grub, mainly, but he's even took a woman or two. I hear he treats 'em rough for a while,

10

uses 'em, and turns 'em over to the madams out there. They could come back, but they don't want to, not after what Anders has done to 'em."

"And nobody's tried to stop him?"

"Hell, yes. Willie Lawrence did, after Anders took off his wife, and look what happened to poor old Willie."

"I wasn't here," Fargo reminded Buck, who was getting a little drunk and maudlin by this time.

"Well, it's just as well. Wouldn't have been anything you could do about it. Nobody did anything about it. That's what was wrong here. Even somethin' as bad as that couldn't get people riled up enough to go after Anders. Except for Willie. He went after him, the poor bastard."

Buck pushed his glass forward. Fargo refilled it.

"It was Hap Tolliver who went by Willie's place a couple of days later," Buck said. "There was a wooden box sittin' on the front porch. Two or three old cats was sniffin' around the box and lickin' at the sides. Hap opened it up and like to died hisself when he took off that lid and saw Willie's face lookin' back up at him." Buck took a drink. "That's when the town got together and hired Stuver."

"Has Anders been back since then?"

"Not yet, but he will be. That's his way. He'll be tired of Willie's wife by now and wantin' somebody else, so he'll come lookin'. He ain't scared of this town. He ain't scared of Stuver. He ain't scared of the devil hisself."

It was an interesting story, and it sounded to Fargo like the town of Fort Benton might be in for some tough times. But it wasn't the Trailsman's problem. He was going back to St. Louis to find another job as soon as possible.

A good part of the evening had passed, and the bottle was just about empty, mostly Buck's doing. Fargo didn't mind. Listening to the old man talk had been as good a way to pass the time as any, and better than most.

"It's getting late," Fargo said. "You can have the rest of the bottle."

"Mighty kind of you," Buck said, reaching for it. He might have been slightly drunk but his hand was steady. He held the bottle up to the light and shook it.

"Not much left."

"It'll have to be enough," Fargo told him.

"I'll make do. You gonna be around town for a while?"

"Leaving tomorrow," Fargo said, rising.

"Well, you take care, you hear?"

Fargo said he would and left the Silver Slipper, thinking that it was time for him to pay his visit.

He'd taken no more than a couple of steps outside the door when something slammed into the side of his head and knocked him sprawling.

3

"That'll take care of the son of a bitch," Snake said, shoving his pistol back into the sash he wore around his waist. "Help me drag him into the alley."

Possum grabbed Fargo under the arms, and Snake took his feet. After they got him into the alley and dropped him in the mud, they stood looking down at him in the darkness.

Snake was skinny, whip-lean, and ugly, with small eyes set too close together. Besides the pistol stuck in his sash, he carried a knife on a string around his neck.

Possum had big ears, big hands, and big feet. His two front teeth protruded and he had a nose like a snout, which might have explained his nickname. He wore a sweat-stained black hat with an eagle feather stuck in the hatband.

"What're we gonna do with him now that we got him?" Snake asked.

"We can start by kickin' the shit out of him, the bastard," Possum said. "We coulda made some time with that woman on the boat if it hadn't been for him."

"Damn right," Snake said with as much confidence as he'd have had if he'd always gotten his way with beautiful women, which was far from being the case. "Son of a bitch cut us out. Get back outta my way, Possum. I get the first kick."

"We better take his pistol first," Possum said, and he slipped it out of the holster.

"Not a bad gun," Snake said. "You gonna keep it?"

"Hell, yes." Possum stuck the pistol in his belt. "You gonna kick this bastard or just talk all night?"

Snake drew back his leg and kicked Fargo in the side. He liked the way it felt, so he did it again. Fargo groaned and rolled over.

"My turn," Possum said, aiming a kick at Fargo's head.

Fargo had come to enough to move aside, and Possum's kick only grazed him.

"He's wakin' up," Snake said. "We better shoot him."

"Yeah," Possum said. "With his own gun."

He pulled the big .44 and was about to pull the trigger when someone said, "Better not."

Possum and Snake turned around to see a man standing at the entrance of the alley. He was holding a pistol of his own.

Snake looked at Possum. Possum pulled the trigger of Fargo's pistol.

The shot went wide, chipping wood from the side of the Silver Slipper.

Before Possum could shoot again, Fargo, now fully conscious, made his move, swinging his leg and knocking Snake's feet out from under him.

As Snake fell, Fargo rose, bringing his fist straight up from the ground and into Possum's sternum. Rotten breath came out of Possum's mouth as he fell back into the wall of the building behind him, gasping for air that he couldn't seem to get into his lungs. The pistol fell from his fingers.

Snake was quick. He turned to run, but Fargo grabbed his collar at the back of his neck and jerked him to a stop. He spun Snake around and buried the toe of his boot in Snake's groin.

Snake didn't even howl. He folded in the middle, clutched his gut, and vomited onto the ground. A sour smell filled the air as Fargo turned to meet Possum, who staggered forward, still gasping. Fargo clubbed him in the side of the neck with his fist, and Possum fell into the puke puddle. Snake heaved again, all over Possum.

Fargo walked around behind Snake, put a foot on his ass, and shoved. Snake went headfirst into the wall across the alley, hit with a solid *thunk*, and collapsed.

Fargo looked at the two fallen men for a couple of

seconds. He didn't think they'd be getting up for a while, so after retrieving his pistol, he walked away and left them there.

He was a little disappointed in himself. He should have been expecting them to try something and been ready for it. They'd probably followed him to the Silver Slipper and waited for him to come out, and he'd let them catch him unawares, like he was some green pilgrim. He blamed the cheap whiskey and the fact that he'd been thinking about Marian.

"Thanks," he said to the man at the alley's entrance. "I don't think those two will be any more trouble."

"Glad to help out." The man holstered his pistol and extended his hand. "Name's Nick Williams."

Fargo shook with Williams. "I'm glad you happened to come by."

"I was headed for the Slipper," Williams said. "Planning to celebrate a little. I'm getting married in the morning."

"Hey, Fargo," Buck said, coming out of the saloon. "I thought you'd left. Hey, Nick. What're you doin' here?"

"I had to take care of a Possum and a Snake," Fargo said. "Nick was a big help."

"Yeah, varmints do get into town now and then," Buck said. "Most of us don't pay 'em no mind."

"They didn't bother me much, either," Fargo said. "Thanks to Nick."

"You want another drink?" Buck asked.

"You buying?"

"Ain't got the money."

"I'll buy," Nick said. "To celebrate my wedding."

"Sounds fine to me," Buck said. "What about you, Fargo?"

Fargo said he had a little celebration of his own planned and wished Nick a happy marriage.

"Couldn't be anything but happy," Buck said. "Miss Katrina is one fine-looking woman."

"I agree," Nick replied. "How about that drink, Buck?"

"Don't mind if I do," Buck said, and the two of them went into the saloon.

It was still quiet in the alley. Fargo grinned. He didn't think Possum and Snake would be bothering anyone else that night, or maybe for several days afterward.

Fargo had no trouble finding the Cudahy house. There was one street in Fort Benton, on the edge of the business district, where several of the more substantial citizens had built homes. Cudahy's was the first one on the block. The windows were dark except for one that glowed dimly with the light of a lamp trimmed low. Fargo had a feeling he knew whose room that was. He crossed the small yard and looked through the window.

Marian sat in a rocking chair, wearing a robe and doing a bit of embroidery. Her hair was down on her shoulders, but she looked as prim and proper as a schoolteacher thinking about the lesson she'd teach to her eager scholars the next day.

Fargo had a different kind of lesson in mind. He tapped lightly on the window, and Marian looked up. She smiled when she saw him and laid the embroidery aside on the small table where the lamp sat. She got up, crossed to the window, and raised it.

"Do you think you can climb in?" she whispered.

"I can manage," Fargo said, and he did.

As soon as he was inside, Marian shut the window and blew out the lamp. It was dark in the room, but moonlight came in through the window, and it didn't take Fargo's eyes long to get accustomed to the dimness. He had excellent night vision, and he could see Marian almost as well as if she'd left the lamp lit.

He watched as she opened the robe and let it fall off her shoulders. Her breasts weren't large, but they were perfectly formed. The nipples stood out stiffly from her dark areolae. Fargo realized that Marian's nipples weren't the only things that were stiff.

The robe dropped to the floor. Fargo's eyes went to the dark thatch of hair at the V of Marian's trim legs.

"See anything you like?" she asked.

Fargo didn't answer. He started removing his clothing. Soon he was as naked as Marian, his ivory shaft standing at attention.

Marian admired it for a second before taking it in her hand and giving it a few gentle strokes.

"Is that for me?"

Fargo nodded, and Marian sank to her knees on the floor. She used her tongue to lave the head of Fargo's hardness, and then engulfed him with her hot, wet mouth.

She moved her head, at the same time stroking him with her fingers. Soon Fargo was ready to explode, but before he could, Marian stopped and stood up.

"Sit in the rocker," she said.

Fargo moved awkwardly to the rocker and sat down, his eager pointer standing up high from his lap as if it had a life of its own.

Marian turned her back to him and reached for his shaft with her hand. When she found him, she held him steady and started to lower herself onto him. He felt the tip slip inside her, and she stopped there, wiggling it around a little. Fargo enjoyed the sensation, and Marian obviously did, too. Then she slid farther down, and before long he was fully into her and she was seated on his lap.

He reached around her and cupped her breasts, running his fingers lightly over the rock-hard tips.

Marian ground her hips down on him and said, "Rock me, Fargo."

Fargo pushed his feet against the floor to give the chair a start. They rocked back, and at the same time, Marian churned against him. Fargo moved his left hand down to her tangled pubic hair, his finger seeking out the rigid pleasure button in the slick slit.

When he found it, he touched it lightly. Marian gasped and leaned back against him.

They continued to rock. The chair squeaked a bit, and Fargo hoped no one who was sleeping in another room would wake up. His finger worked faster as Marian wiggled on his lap.

"Stop," she gasped after a while, and Fargo planted his feet.

The chair came to a stop, and Marian bounced up and down on him. With each bounce she went higher, until he was almost completely withdrawn from her. Then she sank back with a huge sigh as he slid into her with his entire length.

Marian's sigh was so loud that Fargo was afraid that the sound, along with the squeaking of the rocker, was sure to bring someone to investigate. But even if it did, he was too far gone to stop what he was doing.

Marian was moving rapidly now, and Fargo was helping her. They worked together in a heaving frenzy until Fargo reached the point of no return and could no longer hold back.

Marian didn't want him to. "Now, Fargo! Please! Please! Give it to me now!"

Fargo didn't disappoint her. He gushed hot streams into her, one fast spasm after another, as Marian enjoyed her own climax, shuddering from head to foot.

When it was over, Fargo leaned back in the chair, and Marian fell back against him.

"Are you sure you can't stay here in Fort Benton?" she asked after a while. "I think you'd like it."

"I know I'd like it," Fargo said. "But I can't stay."

"I know what you think. You think you have to be out on the trail somewhere, don't you?"

Fargo admitted it.

"Haven't you ever thought about settling down, staying in one place, maybe having a family?"

Fargo had never really considered those things, and he said so.

"Why not?" Marian said. "I thought everybody wanted those things."

"Not everybody. Some folks are better suited to a different kind of life. I'm one of them."

"Well, then, if that's the way you feel about it, I guess I'd better give you something to remember me by. You'd like that, wouldn't you?"

"I sure would," Fargo said. "What did you have in mind?"

"I'll show you if you want me to," Marian said.

Fargo said that sounded like a good idea, and Marian showed him.

4

Fargo woke up in his cabin on the *Chippewa* the next morning with a good appetite, maybe because of the exercise from the previous evening. And not just the exercise with Marian. His ribs were bruised where he'd been kicked, but they weren't paining him too much. He got up, got dressed, and left the boat to have something for breakfast.

Since he didn't know of any other places to eat, he went back to the Big Strike. The tables were crowded this time, and he figured the breakfast might be better than the meal he'd eaten there previously.

It was. He had ham, eggs, and plenty of coffee. By the time he'd finished, he didn't feel the bruises at all. He still remembered Marian, however.

As he was leaving the café, he heard shooting. People started clearing off the streets, and while they were still trying to get out of the way, Fargo heard pounding hoofbeats. He looked to his left as six or eight mounted men raced around the corner. One of them had a woman slung across his saddle. All the men were firing shots into the air and yelling as they rode, dirt and mud flying from under their horses' hooves.

The woman's mouth was contorted, but the sounds of the shots and the running horses drowned out the sound of her screams. The riders were past and gone before Fargo could really get a good look at any of them, or at the woman, but he thought he recognized two of them. Possum and Snake.

Across the street was a woman who hadn't quite gotten out of the way. One of the horsemen had bumped her and knocked her down. Several men were helping her to her feet. She didn't appear to be hurt too badly, but that was just luck. The riders wouldn't have cared if they'd run right over someone. They might not even have noticed.

Fargo thought he knew who the leader of the men must have been, and his suspicions were confirmed when he heard some of the people nearby muttering about Whit Anders.

More men came running along the street behind the fleeing horses, shouting as they ran. One of them, Fargo saw, was Buck. He stopped Buck and asked what had happened.

"It's that goddamn Anders," Buck said. "He's killed Nick. Shot him down right at the church where he was gonna get married."

"Nick Williams? The man who helped me last night?"

"The very one, and that ain't the worst of it. He's carried off Katrina Waggoner, the girl Nick was gonna marry. I knew the bastard would get tired of Willie's wife, and now that he's done it, he's gonna ruin another woman."

"Did anybody try to stop him?"

"Hell, yes, but he was there and gone so fast that we couldn't do no more than pop off a few shots at him."

"What about the sheriff?"

"Somebody's gone to tell him. He'll try to get up a posse. Might not be able to, though. Or maybe he will. Ever'body liked Nick. Ever'body liked Katrina, too. Maybe this time Anders has gone too far."

Fargo had dealt with men like Anders before. They never considered what they did as going too far. They believed they could do whatever they wanted to do as long as nobody could stop them. And they never thought anybody could stop them.

"Will you be in the posse?" Fargo asked.

"You're damn right, I will."

"So will I," Fargo said.

"How come? You didn't know Nick."

"I knew him well enough," Fargo said, and it was true.

Nick Williams had stepped in when Fargo was in trouble without knowing or caring who Fargo was, and he hadn't worried about his own safety. Fargo felt like he had an obligation to return the favor. It didn't matter that Williams was dead. An obligation like the one Fargo had wasn't ended by the death of one of the parties, especially since two of the men who'd been with Anders when he killed Williams were Possum and Snake. When Fargo had been threatened by those two, Nick had stepped in. Fargo hadn't been around to help Nick, but maybe he could do a little something by way of revenge for the dead man.

"You right sure you want to ride out against Anders?" Buck asked. "Your head might come back in a box without the rest of you."

Fargo shook his head. "I'm not worried about that."

"Well, you damn sure oughta be."

"Just tell me where the sheriff's office is," Fargo said.

"Hell, that's where I'm headin'. I'll show you where it is. We might as well both get kilt together."

"I need to stop by the steamboat dock first," Fargo told him. "I have to change my ticket to one for the next boat."

"Might not need any ticket," Buck said. "Not after Whit Anders gets through with you."

"You're a real bundle of sunshine—you know that?"

"I know Whit Anders," Buck said. "That's what I know."

Sheriff Rex Stuver was crazy. Fargo could see that from the minute they met. The man was practically foaming at the mouth. Something had pushed him over the line.

Fargo and Buck stood with a group of men in front of the little makeshift jail that served Fort Benton. Stuver was telling them what he was planning for Anders.

"We're gonna catch the son of a bitch and shoot him down like a dog," Stuver said. His eyes glittered in his weathered face. "You don't have to worry about bringing him back here for any trial."

"What if he gives himself up?" a man asked. "We can't very well shoot him then."

Stuver spit a yellow gob on the ground to show what

21

he thought of that. "If he gives up, we'll give him a trial right on the spot and string him up. He'll never spend a night in this jail."

"Just as well if he don't," someone said. "My grandma could bust out of that place."

The men all laughed, but it was a nervous laughter. Fargo could tell that they were worried about the consequences of going up against Anders.

"Stuver was in love with Katrina, too," Buck said to Fargo. "Nick Williams beat his time with her, but you can bet the thought of what Whit Anders will do to her is eatin' him up on the inside."

On the outside, too, Fargo thought, looking at Stuver's mad eyes, sunk deep in his weathered face. Fargo didn't like the idea of having a crazy man lead him on a chase after Anders, but he didn't see any way out of the situation, not if he wanted to repay his debt to Nick Williams.

"You men get your horses and meet me back here in half an hour," Stuver said. "We can't be wasting any more time. Anders won't be—you can bet on that."

The small group broke up, and Fargo asked Buck where he could get a horse.

"I keep my mount in a corral close to the livery stable. You could prob'ly rent one there. Buy one if you want to, but it wouldn't be cheap."

"I don't want to buy one. I have a horse."

Fargo thought of the big Ovaro stallion he'd left at a livery in St. Louis. He hoped the animal was being taken good care of.

"We'll get you something you can ride," Buck said. "Come on."

Fargo followed Buck down the street. They hadn't gone far before Buck said, "Can you use that gun you're carryin'?"

Fargo nodded. "If I have to."

Like the Ovaro, Fargo's big Henry rifle was back in St. Louis, which meant he'd be riding out after a dangerous killer armed with a .44 pistol and an Arkansas toothpick. Maybe Stuver wasn't the only one who was crazy, Fargo thought.

"That's good, 'cause you'll have to use a gun, for sure. I know most of those fellas that were at the jail, and there's not a gunhand amongst 'em. They're friends of Nick's, and good fellas, too, every one of 'em, but they're storekeepers and farriers and the like. I'd bet half of 'em don't come back from this little trip we're gonna take."

Fargo didn't take the bet. He asked, "What about you? What're you doing in Fort Benton?"

Buck laughed. "Drinkin'."

"That's a poor occupation."

"Wasn't always what I did. I was one of the first out here, back when this was just a tradin' post and not much more. Trapped around here for many a year. All that's about played out now, and I'm too stove up to do it, anyhow. I managed to hang onto a little money, so I get by."

"You don't spend a lot," Fargo said, remembering who'd paid for last night's drinks.

Buck grinned, showing how few teeth he had. "I like to let other folks buy the drinks when I get the chance. Makes 'em feel good, helpin' out an old codger, and it lets me spend what little money I have on other things. Like a place to stay and some grub now and then."

It seemed like a pretty good financial arrangement to Fargo.

"What do you do for a livin'?" Buck said. "You don't look like the town type."

Fargo told him.

"The Trailsman, eh? I've heard of you. Seems like you get into a little scrape now and then."

"Not if I can help it."

"Some people can't help it. You must be one of 'em. This'un with Anders might be the worst you've been in, though."

Fargo didn't have anything to say about that, but they'd reached the livery barn and the conversation came to an end.

It was cool and dark inside the barn. Fargo smelled hay and oats and horse manure.

While Buck got his mount from the corral, Fargo made a deal to rent a good-looking pinto that reminded him a little of the Ovaro.

"Cost you plenty extra if you don't bring him back

in good shape," the owner said after they'd concluded the deal.

"What if Fargo don't come back a'tall?" Buck asked, walking into the barn leading a flop-eared mule. "Ever think about that?"

"I've thought about it," the liveryman said. "He looks like a man that comes back."

"Never can tell about that," Buck said. "You ready, Fargo?"

"Let me throw a saddle on the pinto," Fargo said.

"Saddle's extra," the owner said. "We didn't talk about that."

"How much?"

The owner told Fargo, and he paid. When they left the barn, Fargo said, "That's about the sorriest-looking mule I ever saw."

Buck agreed. "Agnes don't look like much, but she gets me where I want to go." He paused. "And plenty of places I don't want to go. Like Sundown."

"You don't sound happy about the trip."

"I ain't. I said those men at the jail were storekeepers and the like, good fellas but not much good with a gun. Want to bet me that half of 'em don't show up when it's time to ride out?"

Fargo shook his head.

"You won't ever bet with me," Buck said, "but I don't blame you. You'd surely lose. Those men have thought things over by now, and they'll decide that maybe Nick was a good friend but that he's dead now, and they'll be dead, too, if they go up against Whit Anders."

"What about the woman Anders took?"

"Too late for her," Buck said with a shake of his head. "If I know Anders, he'll have her raped before we ever get to Sundown."

"No wonder Stuver's gone crazy."

"Yeah," Buck said. "First he loses her to Nick, which was bad enough, and now Anders has her. It don't get any worse than that."

"You think Stuver can get the job done?"

"I guess we'll find out, won't we."

"I guess we will," Fargo said.

5

Whit Anders was a big man, and hairy as a bear. Tufts of black hair stuck out from under the cuffs of his shirt-sleeves. His heavy beard all but obscured his eyes. He sat in a chair in one of his saloons, which, like three others in Sundown, had no name. They didn't need names. They all belonged to Anders, except one, and they were all the same. The only differences were the dirt on the floor and the faded women who were there to please the men.

The saloon was noisy with talk and laughter. There was no piano player, however. Anders had shot the last one because he'd played something Anders didn't like, and nobody else had volunteered to take the job. Most likely there was nobody else in town who could play. Piano playing wasn't a skill much in demand in a place like Sundown.

Possum and Snake sat at Anders' table. They were both drinking whiskey, and their eyes were bright with enjoyment of the whiskey and the day's adventure.

"You boys have a good trip up the river?" Anders asked.

He didn't say it loud, but his voice was nevertheless easily heard above the hubbub.

"Tolerable," Snake said.

He didn't mention the run-in with Fargo on the boat, nor did he say anything about the one in town, not figuring there was any need for Anders to know about things like that.

"Didn't make no profit, though," Possum said, admiring the amber color of the whiskey in his glass. "Wasn't any gambling, and wasn't nobody to rob."

"You didn't need to rob anybody," Anders said. "Where would you hide out?"

"Not much place on a boat," Possum agreed. "Don't look like any prospect for you, either, not for a while."

Possum and Snake had taken the boat instead of traveling overland to get to Sundown because Anders had sent them to St. Louis for that purpose. He was thinking about river piracy as a sideline now that the steamboat was coming to Fort Benton, and he wanted to know if it would be profitable.

"The miners are mostly broke, carryin' just enough money for a grubstake," Snake said. "If they even got that much. Some of 'em must be hopin' to get by on their looks."

"Gamblers ain't no better," Possum said. "They're hopin' to skin the miners that strike a vein or pan some color, but they ain't carrying much themselves."

"Proper folks might have money, but there ain't many of 'em," Snake said. "Slim pickins all around."

"What about the mining supplies?" Anders asked.

"You could maybe steal 'em, but it'd be more trouble than it's worth. You get 'em, then you got to get rid of 'em. That might not be easy."

Anders considered the information they'd given him. It looked like river piracy was out for the time being. He'd have to wait till the boat started carrying gold back down the river, or if the gold was shipped out on wagons, he'd steal from the wagons. That's if there was any gold.

"Speaking of skinnin' the miners," Snake said, "you remember that Injun woman you skint that time on the plains? That was something. I bet Possum remembers it, don't you, Possum?"

Possum grinned and took a drink. His Adam's apple bobbed when he swallowed.

"We had us some good times in those days," he said, putting his glass on the table.

"These are good times, too," Anders said, looking around the saloon.

"You gonna skin that woman you took this morning?" Possum asked, a hopeful note in his voice.

"There's other kinds of good things," Anders said. "A town like this is a good thing."

"Yeah," Snake said. "It's good because you run it."

"It's not good for just me, though. It's good for everybody here. It's a place where we can do as we please without having to worry about the law."

He didn't add that people had to worry about him. There were times when he could be worse than any law. The piano player would have testified to that if he'd been aboveground.

"Yeah, this is a good place," Possum said. "But what about the woman?"

"I took that woman, and she's mine. You just forget about her. There's plenty of other women here you can have your fun with."

That was true, and Possum knew it. The thing was, those women didn't look like the other one. They were hard-looking, like they'd seen too much, done too much. There were none of your young, sweet-faced soiled doves in Sundown. Every one of the whores in the outlaw town had long ago lost every bit of innocence and any hope of being anything but a whore.

On the other hand, the woman Anders had snatched at the little church in Fort Benton was young, pretty, fresh as a prairie flower. Not that she'd be that way for long, not with what Anders must have had in mind for her. Even if he didn't plan to skin her, her life in Sundown wasn't going to be a pleasant one.

"If you ain't gonna skin her," Snake said, "what are you gonna do with her?"

Anders laughed, a deep, rolling sound from down in his chest.

"Hell, Snake, do I really have to tell you? Surely that time you served in prison didn't make you forget all you know about what to do with a woman, did it?"

Anders laughed at his joke, and Possum joined in.

Snake didn't see anything funny about it. "I ain't forgot," he said. "I didn't develop no other kinds of interests, either, if you're thinkin' that. By God, if you're

27

gonna poke that woman, why don't you just do it? What the hell are you waiting for?"

"You know what your trouble is, Snake?" Anders said.

"I don't guess I do. But I figure you're about to tell me."

"That's right. I am. Your trouble, yours and Possum's, is that you're impetuous. You know what that means?"

"Nope. I don't have much use for fancy words like that."

Neither Snake nor Possum could read or write. Education had never had any appeal for them.

"It means you rush into things," Anders said. "It means you never learned the pleasures of anticipation. You don't know what that means, either, do you."

Snake didn't bother to deny it, but this time Anders didn't explain. He said, "The thing is, people in Fort Benton are likely to be a little impetuous, too. We killed one of their citizens, and we stole his bride to be. You think they'll just sit back and let us get away with that?"

"They always do," Possum said.

Anders shook his shaggy head. "This is different. We've never just ridden in, killed a man, and snatched a woman from right in front of them. They won't stand for that. They'll think they have to do something about it."

"You believe they'll come after us?"

"Damn right they will," Anders said. He stood up. "They're probably starting out right about now. And you know what that means, don't you?"

"Yep. It means we gotta get ready for 'em."

Anders nodded his approval.

"See there?" he said. "You boys ain't as dumb as you think you are."

Buck had been right about the men not returning to the jail to go out with the posse. No more than half of them had showed back up at the jail. Nobody there blamed the ones who didn't. Everybody knew they were riding into real trouble and might not be coming back, and that staying home was a reasonable thing to do. The only one who seemed to be looking forward to going after Anders was the sheriff, and he didn't appear optimistic about their chances.

He stood in front of the jail and looked the group over, shaking his head.

"Ten men," he said. "Ten men to go up against Anders and his killers. Well, we're not likely to find any others, so you'll have to do."

"What kind of a chance do you reckon we got?" someone asked.

"Better than no chance at all," Stuver answered. He put a foot into a stirrup and swung up into his saddle.

"What he means is, we ain't got a chance in hell," Buck said to Fargo in a whisper. "That's what we ain't got."

"We gonna just ride into Sundown and start blazing away?" the same man asked.

"We'll decide on our tactics when we get there," Stuver said.

Not a good idea, Fargo thought. It was better to have a plan in mind before you started out. But he kept his thoughts to himself.

They rode out of town and along the river. Fargo had seen some of the Breaks on the trip to Fort Benton. The trappers had called them the *Mauvaises Terres,* which Fargo understood to mean the Bad Lands. It was in a way more like a desert than land along a riverbank. It was broken by rocks and hills and cliffs that extended far back from the river.

Bad Lands or not, Fargo was glad to be out in the open country for a change. After being cooped up on the boat and then in the town, he felt a sense of freedom in the wild scenery that had been missing from his life for too long.

The trail wasn't a good one. Fargo thought they would have done better in the steamboat than on horseback, but he was happy to be outside with the wide blue sky overhead, no matter what the circumstances. He could almost forget that they were going after a very dangerous man with people who had little or no experience at fighting.

"Goin's a little rough," Buck said, breaking into Fargo's thoughts. "Won't bother Agnes none, but it might hinder that pinto of yours."

The pinto, however, had no trouble on the rocky trail, and none of the other horses seemed bothered. A couple of miles outside of town, they turned off onto a wider, better-kept trail—the one leading to Sundown.

"Anders don't want to make it too hard to get to his town," Buck said. "He needs the customers for his saloons."

"Seems to me the law would come and drag him out of there," Fargo said.

Agnes snorted as if in reply. Buck laughed.

"The law don't seem interested in botherin' Anders. The Breaks are a long way from anywhere important, and they're hard to get into and out of. That's why they've been a place for outlaws to hole up over the years. The only difference now is that Anders has got things organized."

Fargo was beginning to wonder what he'd gotten himself into. He'd known it was going to be rough, but now he thought it might prove to be suicidal.

"Anybody you know ever been there?"

"Sure. It's not dangerous if you're not part of a posse. If you're on the run or got money to spend, Anders might even be glad to see you."

"How hard will it be for us to get in?"

"That depends."

"On what?"

"Well, this here is the only road into town. The place has some mighty big rocks on three sides of it. Be hard to get to it from those three sides, so we gotta go in this way."

"So it depends on whether Anders is expecting us and what kind of surprise he might have waiting," Fargo said.

Buck nodded. "That's about the size of it," he said.

6

Katrina Waggoner had stopped crying hours ago. Now she was just angry.

She was angry that Nick had been killed, angry that she'd been snatched away from her wedding, and angry that she'd been locked in a room in some whiskey-smelling saloon in Sundown, where she was supposed to wait until some hairy animal named Whit Anders came upstairs, tore her clothes off, and had his way with her.

Well, if that was what he thought would happen, she told herself, he had another thing coming.

Katrina had been born in St. Louis, but she'd lived in Fort Benton for most of her life. Her father had done some trading with the Indians, done a little trapping, done a little of everything to make a living for himself, Katrina, and her mother. Both parents had died of a fever the previous winter, but before they died Katrina had found Nick. Her parents had taken some comfort in knowing she'd have someone to help her get through things, but now even Nick had been taken away.

By Whit Anders. And Katrina was determined to do something about it.

She looked around the room for what seemed like the thousandth time, hoping to see something she hadn't noticed previously, something that would help her get out of there or that she could use as a weapon.

There was nothing. The room was bare except for the bed, and she knew the purpose Anders intended to put that to if he got the chance.

Katrina sat on the bed and listened to the men whooping it up in the saloon. She wondered if Anders was one of them. No doubt he was.

She looked out the window. The room was on the second floor, and all she could see was the unpainted wall of the building next door. There was a narrow alley between the buildings, but no stairway. Anders wasn't going to let her get away that easily.

She was wearing her wedding dress, which she'd made herself. It was white satin, with lace ruffles at the neck and petticoats under the full skirt, dirty now from her ride from Fort Benton. Her veil had been lost somewhere along the way to Sundown—not that she cared about that, not now.

She wore a chemise under the satin top, and over the chemise was a corset. Anders would have plenty of trouble getting her out of that, she thought.

Or he would if she stayed around waiting for him to appear, and she didn't intend to do that.

She got up and crossed to the window. She pushed it upward and, to her surprise, it moved. She'd thought it might be nailed shut, but she supposed Anders didn't think she'd jump. He was wrong.

Sticking her head out the window, she looked down into the deserted alley. It wouldn't be much of a drop, she told herself, not if she hung from the window ledge by her hands.

She pulled her head inside the room. If the window was the only way out, that was the way she'd go, but first she had to do something about her dress.

She reached around and untied the laces in back, then unlaced the top. She kicked off her shoes, removed the dress, then the petticoats, and finally the corset. Standing in the room in her chemise, she thought about how she'd look fleeing through the streets of Sundown.

"I'll probably be attacked by ten men before I go a block," she said aloud.

Although the room lacked a mirror, she knew that she was attractive, with long legs, full breasts, and long black hair. She was the kind of woman that men appreciated, and the men in a place like Sundown would appreciate her more than most, especially if she was wearing just a chemise.

She thought about putting the wedding dress back on,

but it was too bulky to move quickly in. Besides, she thought, anybody in Sundown seeing a woman in a wedding dress would immediately know something was wrong. She'd just have to take her chances in the chemise.

Katrina was a good rider. If she could just get to the street and find a fast horse, she might be able to get out of town. If someone shot her, well, that would be a better fate than what Anders had in mind for her.

She moved to the window and put a leg outside. Turning and grabbing the sill, she got both legs out and lowered herself until her arms were stretched to their full length. Her bare legs scraped against the side of the saloon. She glanced down, checking the distance, and let go.

The alley was hard-packed earth, and she was jarred a little when she landed. She didn't fall, however, and she reached out a hand to steady herself against the building. Then she glanced around.

One end of the alley opened onto the street. The other end led to a larger alley that ran behind the buildings. Katrina decided to go in that direction, thinking that she would be less likely to be seen.

When she reached the alley, she again looked in both directions. There was nothing much to see except for garbage and outhouses. She'd just about decided to go to the left when she heard a door open on the right. She ducked back out of sight, then peeked around the corner.

A woman was standing in the alley, rolling a cigarette. She wore a blue dressing gown, and one look at her was enough to tell Katrina her occupation.

Would the woman help her, or would she call Anders? Katrina had no way of knowing, but there was at least a small chance that she'd help. That was better than no chance at all.

Katrina turned the corner and walked toward the woman, a not unattractive blonde with a painted face. The paint didn't quite cover a knife scar on her left cheek. The blue gown she wore was dirty and torn. Katrina hadn't gone more than a few steps when the woman turned and saw her.

"What the hell are you doing here, honey?" the woman asked, blowing out a stream of white smoke. She eyed the chemise. "Looking for a job? If you are, I'll be happy to take you in. I think the boys here would go wild over you."

Katrina blushed. "I'm not looking for a job. I'm looking for a way out of town."

"Goddamn. You must be that woman Anders stole from Fort Benton. You're the first one ever had the gumption to get out of that room of his."

Katrina didn't say anything.

"He won't like it that you got away," the woman said, taking another puff of her cigarette. "But you won't get far, 'specially dressed the way you are. Anders'll catch you for sure, and then he'll beat you worse than usual when he gets you back in that saloon."

Katrina didn't like the sound of that. Not at all.

"I thought you might help me," she said.

The woman laughed. "Help you? Jesus, honey, he'd kill me if I did that. I kinda like living." She looked down at the shabby gown she wore and then gestured back at the building behind her. "I'll grant you, it ain't much of a life, but it's the only one I got."

"I have money."

The woman looked her up and down, taking her time, as if looking for unexpected bulges under the thin chemise.

"Where might you be hiding it?"

"Back in Fort Benton, I mean, at my house. I could pay you after I get back there."

"Well, now, money's nice, but what I like is money in the hand, not money back in Fort Benton. Besides, living's better than money, no matter what kind of life you have. And the odds of you getting back to where that money is are between slim and none."

Katrina didn't know what to say next. She couldn't think of any other way to appeal to the woman, who puffed her cigarette contentedly.

"I'm sorry I bothered you," Katrina said, and turned to go back the way she'd come.

"Hell, don't take it so hard," the woman called after her. She had a speculative look. "I've thought it over. It

34

might be fun to give Anders a little hell for a change, instead of him giving it to me. Let me think on it some more."

Katrina turned back and waited. The woman smoked, staring off at nothing in particular. After a few seconds, the woman threw her cigarette butt to the ground.

"My name's Slash," she said to Katrina. She touched her face. "For the scar."

Her eyes changed a little when she mentioned the scar. They had been clear and blue, but now they were clouded with something that Katrina thought must be remembered pain.

"I'm Katrina," she said.

"That's a sweet name, but we'll have to think of another one for you. Nobody around here has a name like that, at least not that she'll let anybody call her. You come on inside, honey, and meet the girls."

Katrina wasn't at all sure she wanted to meet anybody, but she couldn't think of anything else to do. The woman opened the door, and Katrina followed her inside.

7

Whit Anders wasn't thinking about Katrina at the moment. He was waiting for the posse that he was sure would soon be arriving from Fort Benton. He was looking forward to their arrival, because he'd be ready for them.

It had been quite a while since he'd irritated anyone in the town enough to get them out to Sundown after him. Some of them came for gambling and whoring, but nobody was interested in trying to bring him to justice for anything he'd done.

Today, however, was different. Today was the first time he'd killed somebody. In Fort Benton, that is. He'd killed Willie Lawrence when Lawrence came after his wife, and he shouldn't have sent that head back to town. He'd thought that might rile people up against him, but they were too cowed to do anything.

The killing of Nick Williams was different, though. It had happened right there in town, and it would be enough to get at least a few people in Fort Benton stirred up enough to come looking for him, he was sure.

And from what he'd heard, the sheriff had once had his eye on Katrina Waggoner. Anders didn't blame him. She was a mighty pretty woman, and he was going to enjoy giving her a good, rough poke when the time came. It would be even better if he had to wait for it, though. That's what men like Snake and Possum would never understand.

He stood on the porch of the saloon and looked at the men who'd gathered in the street after he'd sent Possum for them. There were twenty of them, which he judged would be more than enough to take care of any posse they could raise in Fort Benton. They'd be lucky if they got ten men to come to Sundown. Anders wondered what would happen if he killed all ten of them. The town might get worked up enough to come after him in force, but he didn't think so. The people who lived there weren't gunmen. They didn't know how to deal with violence, not the kind Anders could visit on them.

Even if he was wrong about them and the whole town came after him, Anders wouldn't be too worried. Thanks to the protection of the surrounding rock structures, his town was practically impregnable. Anyone coming into it would have to use the single road, and Anders had put up a couple of double-thick board fences along both sides of it. There were holes cut in each wall so that a rifleman could hide behind them and pick off any rider he wanted to from relative safety, assuming a rider was stupid enough to let him.

Anybody who got past the fence and into the town would have to ride between two of Anders' saloons. He sent eight of the men to the saloons, four to each one.

"Get up on the second floor and take the windows," he said. "If any of those bastards get into town, make sure they don't get any farther."

After the eight men had left, Anders led the others out of town and stationed them behind the walls, six to each side of the road. He put Snake in charge of one side and Possum in charge of the other. Those two weren't exactly soldier material, but they could give the order to fire. That was all Anders needed from them.

Anders hadn't made any attempt to hide the fences. If anybody Anders didn't want in Sundown was crazy enough to try riding past them, that was fine with him. They'd never ride anywhere else.

It was getting on toward the middle of the afternoon, and some of the men were thirsty. Anders made sure they were provided with a little whiskey. Not enough to make them drunk, even though some of them were half-way there already. Just enough to take the edge off.

"Where you gonna be?" Snake asked Anders after he had his men lined up behind the fence.

"I'll be in the saloon."

"Gettin' you some from that woman?"

Anders' face reddened. "You got a big mouth on you, Snake. You might oughta think about that."

Snake looked down at the dirt under his feet. "I didn't mean nothin' by it, Whit."

Anders took a deep breath. He said, "Maybe not. Anyway, you ought to know better. I'll be waiting there for anybody that gets that far."

"Won't be anybody."

"That's the way to talk. But come to think of it, I'd like it if you let one of them through. The leader. That'll be the sheriff unless I miss my guess. We'll make an example of him. I'll stop and tell the boys at the saloons."

"You sure you want to do that?" Snake said.

"I told you, didn't I?"

"Yeah, you did."

"Then that's the way I want it."

"Yeah. You want me to tell Possum?"

"I'll do it," Anders said. "You just get ready."

"I don't see anybody coming," Snake said.

"You will," Anders told him. "Any minute now."

As soon as they got close enough to see Sundown, Fargo knew they were in trouble. The country was rocky and deserted, but the town was situated so that they were going to be funneled into it, right down the one main street. If they got caught in a cross fire in the street, they'd all be killed. He told Buck what he was thinking.

"Yep, could happen like that, all right. But how else we gonna get in there and bring out Katrina?"

"There must be another way," Fargo said.

"Well, you tell that to Sheriff Stuver. He's leadin' this little huntin' party."

Fargo kneed the pinto and rode up beside Stuver. The man's eyes were burning a hole deep into his face, and Fargo knew he wouldn't be able to talk sense to him. That didn't mean he didn't have to try, however.

"I think we're riding into a trap, Sheriff," he said. "If Anders is waiting for us, his men can shoot every one of us out of the saddle before we ever see them."

Stuver turned his burning gaze on the Trailsman as if seeing him for the first time.

"Who the hell are you, anyway?" he said. His voice was tight and strained.

"Fargo's the name. I was a friend of Nick's."

"I don't think I've seen you around Fort Benton."

"I haven't been in town long. But Nick helped me out, and I owe him."

"And I don't really give a good goddamn. I'm leading this posse, not you. You can do what I say, or you can take your cowardly ass back to Fort Benton. Either way, it won't make any difference to me."

Fargo knew he should have known better than to try reasoning with Stuver. He turned back and rode along beside Buck.

"Didn't do no good, huh?" Buck said.

"Not a bit."

"Didn't think it would. Stuver's gone plumb loco."

"Look up there," Fargo said, pointing to the fences that had now come into view. "It's almost like a fort. Anders will have men on both sides of the road. He'll kill everybody that tries to ride past."

"I believe you got it right," Buck said. "Even Agnes here ain't stupid enough to try that."

"Stuver is."

"Yeah, I don't doubt it. A mule's got more smarts than a man whose mind's messed up like his. Wonder how may of these others are messed up as he is? You gonna find out?"

"Let's get a little closer to the town," Fargo said. "Then we'll see."

"There they come." Snake had been looking around the rock, and now he moved behind the fence. "Get ready."

"You think they'll really try to ride right down the road?" someone asked.

"What the hell else they gonna do? Turn tail and go back?"

"That's what they'd do if they had any sense. That's what I'd do."

"It ain't your woman Anders has got locked up in that saloon of his."

"It ain't theirs, either."

"They think it is. Now get yourself ready."

"I'm ready," the man said.

"Good. Let's see how many of them sons of bitches you can kill."

Fargo took in the situation. The fences were blocked on the ends by large rocks that had either been there to begin with or had been rolled into place by Anders and his men, so it was impossible to see who might be waiting for the posse. Not that seeing made any difference. Fargo was certain someone was waiting. He rode up beside Stuver again.

"They're behind those fences. You know it as well as I do. You can't lead these men that way. You'll just get them all killed."

"Fargo—is that what you said your name was?"

Fargo nodded.

"Fargo, didn't I just tell you to get your cowardly ass back to Fort Benton? I don't want to have to tell you again. I'd just as soon shoot you as not and have done with it."

"At least let the men know what they're riding into."

"You go to hell." Stuver pulled his pistol and pointed it at Fargo. "Or maybe you want me to send you."

Fargo didn't have any more to say to Stuver. The other men would have to use their own eyes and brains. He could hear them whispering to one another as he rode back to join Buck.

"Touchy bastard, ain't he?" Buck said when Fargo was beside him.

"That's one way of putting it," Fargo said. "What do you have in mind to do?"

"Me? I'm just an ignorant old turd on a mule. I'll hang back and see what happens."

"I'll do the same thing then. Maybe we can get past after they gun down everybody else."

"Wasn't too long ago you were calling me a bundle of sunshine. Now you're tryin' to be one, too."

Fargo grinned. He was about to say something when Stuver raised a hand to bring the posse to a halt.

When the men had gathered around him and the horses had stopped snorting, Stuver said, "We'll go in at the gallop, and take them by surprise. Remember, everybody in

40

that pestilent hellhole is an enemy. They'll be trying to kill you, so you'd better try to kill them first."

"What about Miss Katrina?" Buck said. "You want us to kill her, too?"

Stuver gave him a look that would wither a cactus.

"You know damn good and well I didn't mean her."

"That's good. You plannin' to ride right by them fences on either side of the road up there?"

"Why not? If you don't think that mule can make it, you can leave right now." Stuver turned his gaze to Fargo. "And take your candy-ass friend with you."

"Might be somebody waitin' behind those fences," Buck said. "Looks like that's what they was built for."

The other men shifted uneasily in their saddles. Leather creaked.

"Leave now if you're scared," Stuver said. "Anybody else who's a chicken-livered coward can go with them."

Nobody said a word. Fargo wasn't sure if they were just stupid or more scared of the sheriff than they were of what Anders might have in store for them.

"Anybody leaving?" Stuver said.

"Hell, no," a man yelled out.

"All right. Let's go, then."

Stuver turned his horse toward Sundown. He drew his pistol and kicked the horse in the sides. It took off in a burst of speed, and the posse followed.

Buck and Fargo watched them go.

"They'll get shot to pieces," Fargo said.

"Yeah, I reckon they will," Buck said. "But I guess they deserve it."

"Nobody deserves it."

"You think we can stop 'em?"

"No," Fargo said. "But I think we ought to try."

"I was afraid you'd say that. Get up, Agnes!"

The mule jolted forward, with Buck's elbows flapping like wings.

Fargo laughed and took off after him.

8

Slash took Katrina through a kitchen and down a hall into the parlor of the whorehouse. There was only one woman there, a redhead who was wearing a chemise even flimsier than the one Katrina had on.

"That's St. Louis Lou," Slash said. "Lou, this is Blue-Eyed Kate." She turned to Katrina. "That all right with you, Kate?"

Katrina nodded. She didn't know what else to do.

"It's a pleasure to make your acquaintance, I'm sure," Lou said in a parody of good manners. She didn't move from the couch where she reclined.

"Kate'll be staying with us for a while," Slash said. "I'll take her up and show her a room."

"She might be too much competition for some of them other whores," Lou said. "Me, I'm not worried."

Lou was plump but firm, with heavy thighs and a thick waist. Katrina didn't think she was very pretty, but maybe she would appeal to a certain kind of man.

Slash, on the other hand, was pretty once you got past the scar. Katrina thought that the blue robe might conceal a very nice figure, too.

"I'm not going to be working here," Katrina said.

"Then what're you gonna do?" Lou wanted to know. "Cook for us? Sweep up after us?"

"You just mind your own business and don't tell anybody she's here," Slash said. "If you know what's good for you."

Lou put on a pouty face. Slash didn't seem to care. She told Katrina to follow her upstairs.

"That's where all the work goes on," she said. "Down here's just the showcase. No customers here now, though. I think a lot of the men are too busy."

"Doing what?" Katrina asked.

"I don't have the least idea," Slash said, but Katrina could tell she was lying. She had a feeling that not much happened in Sundown that Slash didn't know about.

She followed Slash up the stairs, where a hallway was lined on both sides with doors, some of which were open. Slash didn't stop at any of the open ones to make introductions, and Katrina hardly glanced inside. When she did, the listless women inside didn't seem interested in her.

Slash led Katrina to the end of the hall and opened the last door on the right.

"This will be your room," she said, stepping aside for Katrina to enter.

Katrina looked into the room. The interior was dark, and she couldn't really see anything. She felt Slash's hand on her back, and then she was shoved inside. The door closed behind her. She turned around as the lock clicked.

"You make yourself comfortable," Slash said through the locked door. "I'll be back in a little while."

Katrina tried the door handle, giving it a good rattle. The door was locked all right.

"Let me out of here," she said, but there was no answer.

She turned and saw a couple of thin lines of light where there might be a window. There was one, all right, but it had been boarded up, maybe to prevent reluctant recruits into Slash's business from leaving that way. Katrina wasn't a recruit, and she didn't intend to go into the business. It didn't make much difference what she was, however. She wouldn't be escaping through the window.

Her eyes had adjusted to the darkness now. She located a bed and a washstand with a pitcher and bowl on the top. There were no other furnishings in the room.

She was a prisoner again, and this time getting out was going to be even harder.

*   *   *

Fargo and Buck couldn't catch up with the posse, but Fargo didn't think it would make any difference if they did.

Stuver was twenty yards in front of the other men, and when he rode right past the two palisades, Fargo thought for just a second that maybe he'd been wrong about the possibility of an ambush. No shots were fired at Stuver.

Then the other riders reached the fences, and the shooting started. Men and horses screamed and went down. Powder smoke rose in the air.

Two of the men in the posse weren't killed in the fusillade. They managed to get to their feet and fire off a couple of shots at the wall before bullets ripped into them and knocked them down.

Fargo and Buck reined up and watched the slaughter. They didn't have much choice, other than riding on and getting killed themselves.

The slaughter was over almost as soon as it had started. Eight men lay dead, along with a couple of the horses. Several of the other horses milled around, but two of them broke for the town, and the others ran back down the trail to where Fargo and Buck sat on their own mounts.

Fargo saw Stuver turn in the saddle to see what had happened. He wheeled his horse around, but there was firing from the buildings on both sides of him. He was trapped in the street with nowhere to go.

"What're we gonna do?" Buck said. "We can't help him. They'd kill us before we got anywhere close."

"He put himself there, and he got eight men killed," Fargo said. "We might as well go back to Fort Benton until I can figure out what to do next. Unless you have a better idea."

"You just gonna leave Katrina there, with men like that?"

"I don't plan to leave her. I still owe Nick. But getting myself killed won't help her any."

"I know it wouldn't. I just hate to think of what's gonna happen to her."

"You'd do better to worry about what's going to happen to the sheriff. I'd say he's the one in real trouble."

Before Buck could offer an opinion on that, some of the men who had been behind the fence spotted them and opened fire from the cover of one of the rocks.

"Let's light a shuck," Buck said as a bullet whined past, and they got out of there.

Stuver was dumbfounded by the sudden bad turn things had taken. He'd been convinced that he'd ride into Sundown, against all odds, and take Katrina home, where she'd recognize what a mistake she'd made in choosing Nick Williams over him.

That was the way things should've worked out.

Now his posse was dead, except for that gutless Fargo fella and the equally gutless Buck Terrell, and Stuver was responsible. Not only that, but he was stuck in the middle of the only street in Sundown, with guns pointing at him from second-story windows on both sides.

Sweat ran into his eyes as he frantically tried to think of an escape, but every time he made a feint in any direction, a bullet chewed up the ground before him.

After a few seconds of that, Whit Anders walked out onto the porch of the saloon.

"Well, Sheriff," Anders said with a big grin, "you've had quite a welcome to my little town."

"You murdering bastard," Stuver said, raising his pistol.

A rifle fired overhead, and the pistol went flying, along with a couple of Stuver's fingers. Blood spurted out of the stumps that remained.

Stuver looked at his hand in disbelief.

"Better wrap that up," Anders said. "You don't want to bleed to death out there in the street."

Stuver pulled off his neckerchief and wrapped his hand. The pain hadn't started yet, but he knew it would come soon enough.

When the sheriff had his hand wrapped, Anders stepped off the porch and walked over to him.

"Get down off that horse," he said.

Stuver had recovered his nerve. "You go to hell."

Anders laughed. "Not much doubt about that, but I think you'll get there before I do."

He reached for Stuver. Stuver tried to kick him, but

Anders grabbed his leg, while at the same time jumping up and taking hold of his belt with the other hand.

He threw Stuver into the street and stepped on his bloody hand.

Stuver screamed. The pain had arrived.

Anders ground the hand into the dirt, but Stuver clamped his mouth shut. He muffled his groans. Anders stomped on the hand, but Stuver didn't scream again.

Anders kept his foot on the hand and waved for the men in the windows above to come on down. By the time they reached him, Snake and Possum had brought their men back into town and the saloons all over town had emptied out. Everyone gathered around Stuver and Anders.

There was a lot of joshing and laughing, and Anders waited for things to quiet down. When that happened, he said, "Most of you remember what I told you about Sundown. Nobody comes in here unless I say so. A lot of you are paying me good money to stay here, and now you know that it's not wasted. This sheriff came here with blood in his eye, and look at him now. Crawling in the dirt like a worm."

Anders mashed down on the mangled hand, and Stuver squirmed on the ground without making a sound, his eyes shut tight against the pain.

"Yeah, you took care of him, all right," Snake said.

"He didn't come here after me, though," a big man in the back said. "He came after you, Anders. Seems like you're just taking care of yourself."

"If he'd been after you, it would have worked out the same way. Tell 'em about the posse, Snake."

"All dead. Eight of 'em."

"Hear that, Sheriff?" Anders said, looking down at Stuver. "Eight men dead, thanks to you. I hope you're right proud of yourself."

Stuver didn't answer, so Anders raised his foot and stomped on the hand again. Stuver couldn't repress a moan.

"I guess he's not so proud," Anders said.

"What're we gonna do with him?" Snake asked.

"I have an idea about that," Anders told him. "We're gonna make him an example."

"How are we gonna to that?" Snake wanted to know. So Anders told him.

Katrina was horrified at what she'd just seen. At the sound of the shots, she'd gone to the boarded-up window and pressed her face to the boards. Peering through one of the cracks between the boards, she saw what happened to Stuver. It was cruel and inhuman, she thought. Anders was even worse than she'd thought he was.

She watched as two of the men pulled Stuver to his feet. Katrina couldn't hear what they were saying to him, but Stuver seemed to have no reaction. He cradled his mauled hand and stood there, hanging his head.

Katrina had no great affection for Stuver. He'd courted her for nearly a year, and while he'd been gallant and suitably dashing, she'd never cared for him. There was something about him that put her off, some odd wildness in his character that almost frightened her. He'd even pressed her to marry him, but she'd turned him down. Then she'd met Nick Williams and fallen in love.

Stuver had been irate. He couldn't seem to understand how she could possibly choose someone other than him. He'd come to her house and bothered both her and her parents. It was as if she'd never told him the way she felt, though of course she had, putting it as gently as possible.

Stuver had said he loved her and that was all that mattered. He'd gotten very worked up about it. Katrina had been afraid that he might try to hurt Nick, maybe even kill him, but it hadn't come to that.

Now Nick was dead anyway, killed by the man who was torturing Stuver in the street below her window.

Someone in the crowd ran off down the street and returned in only a couple of minutes. He was carrying a rope. He gave it to Anders, who made a noose in it. He put the noose over Stuver's head, and Katrina knew they meant to hang him.

They weren't going to do it right there, however. They prodded Stuver in the back with rifles, and he stumbled off down the street with the jeering crowd following him.

Katrina knew she'd never see Stuver again. Not alive.

47

9

At least one man in Sundown had no interest in the festivities that were going on with Anders and Stuver. His name was Ken Briles, and he sat in his own saloon. Briles had his feet up on a table and a drink in his hand. He was a slick-looking man, almost dudish in his frock coat and tie. He might have been the only man in Sundown who bathed more than once a month.

"You don't want to watch?" Gar Holliman asked.

Holliman sat at the table and played solitaire with a greasy deck of cards. He had worked for Briles for two years. He wasn't exactly bright, but he was tough, and that was all Briles cared about.

"I don't give a damn what they do to that sheriff," Briles told him. "It doesn't affect me or my plans."

Holliman didn't know for sure what plans Briles was talking about, but he had a pretty good idea. Briles didn't like Anders, and he didn't like taking orders from him.

Holliman was pretty sure that Briles would like to be running Sundown for himself, but that wasn't going to happen as long as Whit Anders was around, and there was no way to get rid of him short of killing him, as far as Holliman knew, and nobody was going to get away with that. Not with the kind of men Anders kept around him to watch his back.

Briles put his feet on the floor, took a sip of his drink, and leaned forward on the table. He looked at Holliman's solitaire hand.

"Black queen on the red king," he said.

Holliman placed the card.

48

"Anders is a fool," Briles said.

Holliman nodded. He'd heard it before.

"He lets people on the run stay here for a fee, and now he's trying to get honest people to come in for a drink or a poke, or maybe to gamble away their money at his faro tables. Why would he want to risk it by killing a sheriff?"

Holliman shrugged. Thinking wasn't his strong suit.

"I'll tell you why," Briles went on. "He's risking it because he thinks it'll show how powerful he is. How he's the difference between living and dying in Sundown. But he's a fool because the people in Fort Benton aren't going to let this pass. They'll do something about it. You can count on that for goddamn sure."

"Right," Holliman said.

"And that's just fine with me," Briles told him. "When Anders goes down, there's somebody waiting to take over, somebody that knows how to run this town right."

"Sure," Holliman said, looking at Briles from the corner of his eye. He didn't think that Briles was watching him, so he moved a red seven onto a black nine.

Briles saw the move, but he ignored it. He didn't give a damn what Holliman did. He was still angry that all his customers had left as soon as the shooting started, taking money out of his pocket. It seemed to him that was all Anders did: take money out of his pocket.

And before the shooting started he'd been angry because he didn't have as many customers as Anders did. Being angry was becoming a habit for Briles, and he didn't like it.

If he'd thought it over, he might have admitted that he owed something to Anders. Briles had come to Sundown when he didn't have anywhere else to turn. He'd gotten into some serious trouble in California with the wife of a Spanish grandee, who didn't understand what Briles was doing in his bedroom when he returned home unexpectedly. Briles had been forced to defend himself, and he'd killed the man.

Briles considered it a fair fight, and not even his fault, but nobody else in the town had agreed. The fact that Briles had made off with some of the man's gold didn't help matters any, and the man's relatives had chased

49

Briles out of the state and all the way to Montana. They'd have killed him if they'd caught up with him, but he managed to stay a day or so ahead of them until he found refuge in Sundown. At a price.

The relatives didn't give up just because Briles had eluded them, however. At least one of them was still hanging around in Fort Benton, or so Briles had heard. He'd used some of his gold to pay off Anders, and more of it to make sure that if the relatives were spotted in Sundown he'd get a warning.

Then he'd used most of the rest of the gold to buy a couple of buildings and put in his saloon. He was doing all right, getting his investment back and even making a little profit from it, but he saw himself as doing even more, if he could ever get Anders out of the way.

Getting Anders of the way—that was the problem. Holliman was tough, but not tough enough to take on Anders. And Briles certainly wasn't going to do it himself. He needed more support in the town. A few men were for him, but not the majority.

He wouldn't really need a majority if he could find one really good man, someone who wasn't afraid of Anders, but as far as Briles knew such a man didn't exist.

It was a real problem, and so far he hadn't found a solution. But he would, one of these days. He'd have to, because he knew Anders was a little worried about him, and when Anders got worried about someone, someone was likely to wake up dead one morning.

Briles glanced at Holliman's solitaire hand and saw that Holliman had cheated again. Maybe there was some way to cheat Anders. Or just to get a little advantage on him. There had to be a way. Briles hoped he came up with it soon, before it was too late for him.

Fargo and Buck got back to Fort Benton in the late afternoon. By the time they'd gotten the horse and the mule taken care of at the livery, there were people gathered around, wanting to know what had happened in Sundown and where the rest of the posse was.

That was something that had always puzzled Fargo about towns. News traveled fast in every one of them.

There were times out on the prairie or up in the mountains when weeks could pass without any word from the rest of the world, and that was the way Fargo liked it. If you lived in a town, you couldn't make a move that everybody there didn't know about within minutes.

So many people crowded around them, with everybody talking at once, that Buck yelled, "Dang it, we can't talk with all this hooraw. Come on down to the jail, and I'll tell you all about it."

He headed away, and the crowd followed. Fargo did, too. In a few minutes Buck and Fargo stood where Stuver had addressed the posse only a few hours earlier.

Buck spotted a man in the back of the crowd and said, "Mayor, you better come up here with us. We got some bad news for a lot of folks."

A woman in the front started crying when Buck said that, and someone led her away.

The mayor was a self-important little man in a suit and cravat. He stood beside Buck and said, "Tell your story, Terrell."

Buck looked out at the faces of the people gathered at the jail. "Ain't no good way to tell you this," he said, "except just to spit it out. We're the only two come back, and there won't be any others behind us."

The crowd buzzed at that news. Some of the men shouted, and another couple of women began to cry.

"They killed the sheriff, too?" the mayor asked.

"Don't know for sure," Buck said. "But they had him trapped in town. I don't expect he'll come to a good end."

"What're you gonna do, Mayor?" a man shouted. "We got no sheriff, and Anders has killed nearly a whole posse. You can't let him get away with that. Those were good men he murdered, and our friends."

"And what about you, Buck?" another man yelled. "Why the hell didn't you die with 'em? You get friendly with Anders all of a sudden?"

Buck's face darkened. "You're a low-down dog, James Corbett. If I was within twenty years of your age, I'd come over there and whip your ass."

The mayor raised a hand to quiet things down. "This

51

is something that we need to discuss calmly before we make a decision. I'm calling a meeting of the town council in my office in one hour."

"You'd damn well better do something!"

"We will," the mayor promised, but judging from the look on his face, Fargo figured he didn't have any idea what the something would be.

"Buck, you'll have to come to the meeting," the mayor said.

"What about Fargo?"

"Who?"

"This fella here. He was with us."

The mayor turned to Fargo. "I don't believe I know you."

"Fargo's the name."

"I'm Mayor Carroll." He put out a hand, and Fargo shook it. "Have you been in town long?"

"Long enough to owe Nick Williams. That's why I rode out with the posse."

"Then you'd better come to the meeting, too. One hour, in my office. Buck will show you where it is."

The crowd was breaking up, and Carroll walked through it, or tried to. He could hardly go a step without someone stopping him to ask a question or offer a suggestion.

While everyone was occupied with the mayor, Fargo and Buck slipped away.

"Better get us a bite to eat," Buck said. "My belly's growlin', and that meetin's liable to go on all night. I got some fixin's at my place. Come on."

Fargo followed him down the alley and away from the jail.

The sun was going down in a red-and-orange blaze when they got to Buck's house, which was just a tumble-down shack on the outskirts of the town, nothing more than one room with a little stove, a table, and a bed.

"If you're lookin' for fancy, you came to the wrong place," Buck said when they were inside.

"As long as you feed me, you won't hear any complaints," Fargo said.

"Bacon and beans is what I got."

"Then bacon and beans will be just fine. What about the families of those men who were killed today? Who's going to tell them?"

"You can bet somebody's taken care of that already. The mayor'll see to it if they ain't got the word from somebody else."

Fargo thought again about Stuver and how crazy he'd been. He said, "We should have stopped that sheriff."

"How the hell was you gonna do it? Shoot him? Those fellas could see the same thing we could, and they followed him. We tried to tell 'em. What happened to 'em ain't our fault."

Fargo knew Buck was right, but he couldn't help feeling that he'd been a party to the massacre outside Sundown. He even felt some small responsibility for Stuver, since he'd gone off and left him in Anders' hands.

"I could just go to Sundown," Fargo said. "Tell them I was there for the women."

"Sure you could. And after that little dustup you had with those two fellas last night, I'll bet they'd believe what you told 'em, too."

"Snake and Possum?"

"Yeah. I knew you wasn't talkin' about any ordinary varmints after that scuffle Nick helped you out of, and he told me he'd seen 'em. Those two are in thick with Anders."

Snake and Possum already had it in for Fargo, and he knew they'd like nothing better than a chance to get even with him for whatever it was they thought he'd done to them.

"I guess it's not such a good idea to try riding in there," Fargo said, but he was still thinking about it.

"You guess right. Now you want some bacon and beans, or not?"

"I want it," Fargo said.

"Then get out of the way and let me get busy."

Fargo did as he was told.

10

Anders had Stuver standing in front of the fence on the right-hand side of the road into town. Stuver's hands were tied behind his back, and his ankles were tied together.

Anders checked the noose and tossed the end of the rope over the wall. Snake was on the other side. He caught the rope and pulled it taut. Stuver didn't say a word.

"I've decided to let you go out in style," Anders told him. "Look over there."

Anders pointed to the sunset. The whole sky seemed to be on fire.

"There ain't a prettier sunset in all of Montana, and sundown's the best time of day out here. That's how the town got its name."

Stuver kept silent. Anders looked around.

"Some of you men go back there and help Snake. He's not gonna be able to do this all by himself. Possum, you go on."

"Goddamn," Possum said. "I wanted to watch."

Anders just looked at him. Possum went to join Snake.

"You, too, Grunt."

Grunt was a big, slow-walking, slow-talking man with hands the size of hams. He could probably have stretched Stuver's neck without any help. He didn't question Anders.

"That ought to do it," Anders said when Grunt had disappeared behind the fence. "You want to grace us with any last words, Sheriff?"

Stuver shook his head.

"Mouth's kinda dry, huh? I hear it gets that way when a man knows he's about to go to his final reward. Anybody got a drink for this man?"

A couple of men had bottles. Anders took one and uncorked it. He walked up to Stuver and held the neck of the bottle to the sheriff's mouth.

Stuver clamped his lips tightly.

"You sure you don't want a sip?" Anders said.

Stuver remained silent.

"Might make your hand feel better," Anders said. "Those fingers probably hurt."

Stuver shook his head.

Anders grinned. "You're a stubborn coot."

He put the cork back in the bottle and handed it back to its owner.

"Well, now," Anders said, turning to Stuver again. "I guess you're determined to go out of this life without saying anything at all. I don't mind, but I thought it might do you some good to have your say." He stepped around Stuver and knocked on the wall with his fist. "Hoist him, boys!"

The rope tightened, and Stuver was hauled to his toe tips.

"Wait," Stuver said, his voice a harsh croak.

Anders hit the wall again. "Hold it, fellas."

The rope relaxed just a little. Stuver's face was haggard. His eyes looked like smoldering coals.

"Go ahead, Sheriff," Anders said. "Say your piece."

Stuver cleared his throat, and Anders stepped well away from him. Giving him a contemptuous look, Stuver spit on the ground.

"You've had your fun with me, Anders," he said, his voice grating. "I guess you'll have some more when you kill me. But you won't have things your way always. Sooner or later, you'll run up against somebody who's meaner or smarter or both. I hope the end you come to is no better than mine."

He stopped, and Anders waited a few seconds. Then he said, "That's all?"

Stuver nodded.

"Hoist him, boys," Anders yelled.

The rope tightened, and Stuver was pulled halfway up the wall.

"That's far enough," Anders called.

Stuver hung there gasping for air. Before long, his face darkened. He kicked his bound heels against the wall as if trying to find something to stand on. Finding nothing, he writhed like a wounded snake, flopping against the fence as his neck stretched and he struggled for breath. It was terrible to see, and even some of the men who'd come to watch turned their heads away.

It took a while for Stuver to die, but when it was over he hung slumped against the fence, his head fallen to one side, his tongue protruding, his burning eyes staring at nothing.

"Show's over, I guess," Anders said.

He stepped around the fence and told Snake to tie the rope to a stake that had been driven into the ground. Stuver's body was going to be left where it was, as a warning.

When the rope was tied to his satisfaction, Anders went back out front. Snake and Possum followed him, along with Grunt.

Possum looked at Stuver's grotesque face with approval.

I wished I'd seen it," he said with regret. "How long you gonna leave him there?"

"Long enough that anybody seeing it will think twice about sending another posse in here," Anders said.

"Might not be good for business," Snake said.

"To hell with business, then," Anders said.

Besides Buck and Fargo, there were four others at the meeting of the town council: the mayor, two storekeepers, and the undertaker. One of the storekeepers was George Cudahy.

After Buck had explained what had happened to the posse, the mayor said, "I can understand how it was, and I can see why you and Mr. Fargo turned back. But you have to admit that it looks bad."

"I don't see it that way," Buck told him. "It just shows we got more sense than to follow some crazy man into

56

an ambush. Those others didn't have to do it, but they went ahead. If we'd done it, we'd be dead, and you wouldn't be any the wiser about what Anders had done to us."

"We don't have to worry about any show of cowardice from Fargo," Cudahy said.

He told the others a little about Fargo's reputation, and explained to them that Fargo had escorted his wife and daughter on the *Chippewa*.

"My daughter says that she's never been better taken care of," Cudahy said.

Fargo smiled and said that the job had been one of the most agreeable he'd ever taken on.

"Well, if George vouches for you, I'm sure the rest of us shouldn't have any doubts," the undertaker, a man named Dabney, said. "You and Buck did the smart thing. Those others should have taken heed. Stuver was just plain crazy."

"Maybe he was," the mayor said. "Where does that leave the town, though? Anders will think he can come in here any time he wants to and kill whoever he pleases."

"He wouldn't be too far wrong, would he?" Dabney said.

"We can't have that sort of thing," Cudahy said. "My wife and daughter joined me here because I assured them that Fort Benton was safe and civilized, not some lawless town where people like Anders go unpunished. Hell, I believed that myself until this morning. We have to take some kind of action."

"We could march the whole town against Anders," the other storekeeper said.

"Sure you could," Buck said. "But if you tried that, how many of you do you think'd come back?"

"We have him outnumbered."

"Yeah. But he's got you outgunned. The fellas there in Sundown don't mind killin'. Hell, they do it for the fun of it. How many of you in this room, not countin' Fargo here, ever pulled the trigger on another human bein'?"

The men stirred uncomfortably. No one said anything.

"That's what I thought," Buck told them. "The same

57

goes for just about ever'body in Fort Benton, too. Oh, there's a few have done it, and I'm one of 'em, but there's not many. That kind is all holed up with Anders. You fellas'd wind up just like those that followed Stuver, and so would anybody who rode with you. That is, if you could get anybody to go, which I doubt. You might've noticed that there wasn't a hell of a lot of men willin' to ride with the sheriff. I didn't see any of you there."

There was silence in the room. The councilmen looked at their fingernails, at the ceiling, at the floor—anywhere but at another person.

After almost a minute had dragged by, Buck said, "Anyway, you're forgettin' that this ain't entirely about the sheriff or those men that Anders had killed. It's about Nick Williams and Katrina Waggoner. God knows what Anders is gonna to do her if somebody don't stop him."

The men at the table looked as if they had a pretty good idea of what was in store for Katrina, but nobody offered any suggestions about how to prevent it.

Finally, Fargo spoke up. "One man might be able to get into Sundown and get the woman out."

Buck looked at him. "You're as crazy as Stuver. I thought we'd already talked about how that wouldn't work."

"Hold on, Buck," the mayor said. He looked hopeful. "Let your friend say his piece."

"I might be willing to try it," Fargo said. "But some of the men in that town know me. It'd be mighty tricky."

"We could hire you," Cudahy said. "It's not like finding a trail or making a new one, but it's honest work."

"That's right," Mayor Carroll said by way of encouragement. "We'd pay you the same as we'd pay the sheriff for the time you spent doing the job."

"Pay you double if you get rid of Anders while you're at it," Dabney said.

The others looked at the undertaker.

"It would be worth it," Dabney told them. "And you know it. Well worth it."

Cudahy nodded. "He's got a point."

The mayor gave in. "All right, Fargo, we'll pay you

double if you get Anders. What we really want, though, is Katrina back here safe among us."

Fargo wouldn't have thought of asking for pay, but he'd be happy to take it, assuming he came back to collect, which he figured was a doubtful proposition.

"I'm startin' to think you're as crazy as Stuver," Buck said. "You can't get into Sundown, and even if you can, you won't get back out."

"He won't know unless he tries," Carroll said.

"Bullcorn. He wouldn't last ten minutes in Sundown."

The mayor looked at Fargo. "He could be right. It's your choice."

"I'm going tomorrow morning," Fargo said.

11

Sundown came alive after nightfall. Most of its residents were people who had no jobs to speak of, so they spent their days sleeping and resting up for the evenings. That's when the saloons were the liveliest and when the whorehouses did their best business.

Katrina could hear laughter through the floor of her room, and through the thin walls she could hear the sounds of commercial sex next door.

She had never thought of herself as a prude, and she knew a little about sex herself, but she had never listened to men groaning and straining in the act with someone else. It seemed unnatural and unpleasant to her, not to mention an embarrassing breach of etiquette. She supposed the women who worked there became accustomed to such noises, but she wondered how they could stand the constant, loveless contact with unfamiliar bodies, most of them none too clean. Could anyone become accustomed to a thing like that?

After it had been dark for a while, and after the woman in the next room had entertained three customers, each one more piggish and enthusiastic than the one before, Slash unlocked the door and brought Katrina a cold supper on a tray. The woman Katrina had met downstairs, St. Louis Lou, was there, too. She stood behind Slash, holding a short wooden club. Behind them was a third woman, holding a lamp.

"I'm sorry we can't offer you a better room," Slash said. She set the tray on the washstand. "I hope you don't think we're inhospitable."

"I think you're my jailers," Katrina said. "I'm no better off here than I was with Anders."

Lou laughed at that, and Slash said, "Oh, but you are, much better. If you were still with Anders, he would have raped you a couple of times by now. Both sides, most likely."

"Some gals wouldn't mind that," Lou said, seeing Katrina's horrified look. She grinned. "Some might even like it."

"Well, I'm not one of them," Katrina said.

"Then we're doing you a favor by keeping you away from him," Slash told her. "Anders is probably going wild about now, wondering where the hell you are. I wouldn't be surprised if he paid me a visit before too long. Do you want me to tell him you're here?"

Katrina didn't have to think long about her answer.

"No," she said.

"Then stop thinking you're a prisoner. You're just a guest who's having to stay in one room for a while."

"What are you going to do with me?"

Lou smacked the club against the open palm of her hand.

Slash smiled. "Don't let Lou bother you. She doesn't like you because you're prettier than she is."

Katrina cut her eyes at Lou. "I'm not afraid of her. And you didn't answer my question."

"The answer is that I don't know yet. I might have a use for you, which would be helpful to both of us. If it doesn't work out, well"—Slash shrugged—"I might have to give you back to Anders."

Lou smiled and tapped the club against her palm.

"You go ahead and eat. Ella, bring in the lamp."

The woman called Ella was tall and skinny, with a long, horsey face and stringy black hair. Her breasts were very large for such a thin woman. She put the lamp on the washstand beside the tray and gave Katrina a smile.

"This is Big Tits Ella," Slash said. "I guess you can see how she got her name. We just call her Ella around here. The men like her tits, of course."

Ella kept right on smiling at Katrina as she licked her lips suggestively.

61

"The funny thing is," Slash said, "that Ella don't even like men."

"I do," Katrina said, a little too quickly. "Some of them, anyway."

"Then what with Lou and her club, and Ella with her particular likes, you'd better not try to get out of this room," Slash said. "Not if you know what's good for you. Let's go, girls."

Ella gave Katrina another smile, and Lou made a little salute with the club. Then they preceded Slash out of the room. When she got to the door, Slash turned around.

"Enjoy your supper," she said.

After the meeting, Cudahy insisted that Fargo walk home with him.

"I'm sure Marian would like to see you again," he said.

Fargo knew there was more on Cudahy's mind than his daughter, however, and after they'd gone a short distance, Cudahy brought up the subject.

"I hope you don't think less of me because I wasn't in that posse," he said.

Fargo hadn't given Cudahy much thought, one way or the other. He said, "I can understand how it is for a man with a family to consider."

The truth, however, was that Fargo didn't really understand. He hadn't been part of a family in a long time, and he had no plans to become a part of one, either. Being tied down in one place wasn't something that had any appeal to him.

"What with Marian and her mother just joining me here," Cudahy said, "I didn't feel like I could leave them."

"It's just as well you didn't," Fargo said. "If you had, you wouldn't have come back."

"Exactly. Some people have a gift for survival, and I'm not one of them. You are, though, Fargo, if I'm to judge by what I've heard of you. Even at that, you're taking a mighty big risk if you go into Sundown alone to try to bring Katrina Waggoner back."

There was nothing to say to that, so Fargo just shrugged.

"You must think you owe Nick Williams a lot."

"He helped me out when I was in a tough spot," Fargo said. "I'd have done the same for him if I got the chance, but I didn't. So I owe him, all right."

"We'll all be in your debt if you succeed."

"You're paying me a salary. That's plenty."

Cudahy shook his head as if he didn't understand Fargo at all.

Spending time in a parlor making polite conversation wasn't one of Fargo's gifts, but he did the best he could. Marian kept teasing him with her eyes when her parent weren't looking. Fargo felt a certain pressure building up, and it didn't help him keep up his part of the conversation very well. However, he knew that when he met Marian later, as he was sure he would, there was one thing he wouldn't have any trouble keeping up.

George and Jane Cudahy didn't seem to notice Fargo's inability to enjoy the conversation, and they praised the Trailsman again and again for his bravery. He could tell they considered it foolhardiness, too, but that didn't bother him. He knew what he had to do.

Finally the ordeal was over, and Fargo left.

An hour later he was back at the Cudahy house again and inside Marian's bedroom.

Five minutes after that, Marian lay atop the bed. She was completely nude, her hair fanned out around her head, her eyes closed, and her mouth twisted with the sheer pleasure that she was experiencing.

Fargo was also naked, lying beside his her, running his hands slowly over her body, letting the tips of his fingers explore every inch of her velvety skin.

As his fingertips traveled slowly and lingeringly across the diamond-hard nipples of her breasts, Marian reached out with her left hand and clasped his penis. She began to stroke it gently, exciting Fargo with the desire to plunge it into her. But he resisted because he knew things would only be better for the waiting.

Fargo lowered his head and teased Marian's left nipple with his tongue. She arched her back to meet him, then released his penis and took his head in her hands as she pulled his mouth to hers for a deep, soul-searching kiss.

After they broke apart, she sank back onto the bed and allowed Fargo to continue kissing her, but in different places: her breasts, her navel, the mass of crisp curls below.

Moving even lower, Fargo parted Marian's nether lips with his searching tongue. Marian sighed and forced her hips down to bring his flicking tongue into close contact with her swollen clitoris.

"There!" she breathed. "There."

Fargo's tongue slid up and down, higher and lower, until it slipped easily into the sweet wet heart of her. Marian let out a long moan and reached down to pull his head to her as tightly as she could.

Fargo enjoyed himself for a few moments, as did Marian. Then he raised his head and began working his way back up her long, lithe body. She trembled with desire at every light touch of his lips and tongue.

After several minutes, Fargo got up, sat down astride her, and began rubbing the tip of his penis across her hot, rigid nipples, which seemed to grow even hotter and harder each time he touched them. Marian opened her eyes and smiled up at Fargo. She took his penis in her hands and drew it between her breasts and into her mouth, at first sliding her tongue languorously around the tip and then sucking it deeper and deeper into her mouth as Fargo tried not to explode. It was as if a volcano were about to erupt from the end of his penis. He finally had to pull away because he knew he couldn't last much longer.

When he drew back, Marian turned over beneath him, exposing her magnificently rounded rump, a clear invitation for Fargo to begin sliding his penis up and down the sweet crease that divided the perfectly proportioned cheeks. His penis was so hot that it must have felt like a branding iron, but Marian didn't pull away. She lifted her hips and helped him as he moved up and down, faster and faster.

Almost at once he was near the bursting point again, and he tried to slow himself, but Marian wasn't cooperating. She kept pumping her hips, and her irresistible rear kept rising and falling until suddenly Fargo felt himself nudging at the slickery opening of her vagina. As hot and wet as the opening was, Fargo was too hugely endowed to make an easy entrance. He pushed as gently as he could, and after several sweetly agonizing seconds he felt the tip of his penis slip inside.

When it made its entrance, he felt it clasped hotly and tightly as Marian's vaginal walls contracted on him. Once again he had to hold back, which was almost an impossibility as he was pulled deeper and deeper inside.

"Ah, ah, ah," Marian moaned as her hips began to move, bumping and grinding, swivelling and twisting, as she thrust her ass against him.

Fargo moved, too, back and forth, more and more swiftly, until he was no longer even thinking. All his energies and all his feelings were concentrated in one single part of his being as his back and legs began to stiffen and he could feel everything that had been building up inside him gather itself to pour out in one white-hot stream.

"Ah, ah, ah," Marian cried as she pushed against him, forcing him so deeply into her that they seemed almost to be one two-headed creature.

Fargo reached around and clasped Marian's breasts in his hands, massaging them and rubbing the nipples between his thumbs and forefingers.

Marian threw her head back and her hair swirled around Fargo's face as he began to bump against her even harder, slapping against her buttocks until he was so deep within her that he could go no farther, no matter what. He froze like that for a long, drawn-out second, and then his release began, flowing out of him as if it would never stop.

Eventually it did, of course, and Marian collapsed beneath him. He lay atop her back, still inside her, as they caught their breaths and waited for their hearts to stop racing.

"Are you sure you have to go to Sundown?" Marian said after a while.

"I'm sure," Fargo told her.

"I'd miss you if I never saw you again."

Fargo didn't bother to mention that if he'd gone back

to St. Louis as he'd planned, she'd likely not have seen him again, much less as soon as she had.

"I'll be back," he said.

"Is that a promise?"

"That's a promise," he said.

12

Whit Anders' face was red with anger and frustration. He got even more frustrated when Slash grinned at him.

"You lost a woman, Whit?" she said. "Now how could that happen? I thought women loved you so much they'd never leave you for anything in the world."

"You know what happens when they do," Anders said.

Slash touched the scar on her face. She knew, all right. She'd been one of Anders' women once, but his appetites were exotic, and there'd come a time when she refused to do what he wanted.

She'd walked out on him, but he'd found her and brought her back for her punishment. Sometimes she was surprised that she was still alive, but she was. That didn't mean she was free of Anders, however. No woman in Sundown could say that she was completely free of him. No man, either.

"If you've seen that girl, you'd better tell me," Anders said. "I'll do more than scar you if you don't."

They were sitting in Slash's private room, and Anders kept his voice low and threatening so as not to be heard by any of the other women.

"What would I do with her if I had her?" Slash said.

"You couldn't do anything, but you might think you were saving her from me. If you think that, you're wrong. You'd never get her out of town without me finding out. You for damn sure can't put her to work here."

"You mean you've already broken her in, Whit?"

Slash knew the answer, of course, but she wondered what he'd say.

"No, goddamn it. That's one reason I want her back."

"If she's in town, you'll find her. Maybe Briles has her."

Anders looked like he wanted to spit on the floor at the mention of Briles' name.

"I'm going to his place next. If he's got her, I'll kill him."

"You've been wanting to do that for a while, haven't you. He's still around, though."

"I can't go around killing men who pay me to live here, but this is different. If somebody takes something that belongs to me, I'm not going to stand for it."

You are standing for it, Slash thought, and tried not to smile. It gave her a perverse pleasure to see Anders so worked up.

"You better talk to Briles," she said. "He might know something. I damn sure don't."

Anders stood up and walked to the door. When he reached it, he turned and said, "Your place is a lot closer to mine than his is. Hard to imagine how a woman dressed in her shimmy-tail could get very far in this town without somebody seeing her."

Slash leaned back in her chair, trying to appear relaxed.

"It's hard to explain, all right, but she's not here, Whit, and I didn't see her. Like I told you."

"If you're lying to me, I'll kill you. You know that, don't you?"

"I know you'd try." Slash touched the scar again. "This time, I might be ready for you."

Anders' only answer was a burst of vicious laughter as he left the room.

Ken Briles sat in his usual chair at the back of his saloon and looked out over the evening crowd. The place smelled of whiskey and sweat and tobacco smoke, smells as familiar to Briles as his own heartbeat.

He heard the clink of glasses and the click of poker chips, along with laughter and cursing and talk, both low and loud, all the usual sounds of an evening. Also as usual, there were fewer men gathered in his place than in any of those owned by Whit Anders.

Briles could understand why that was, but he didn't like it. He'd done as much as he could to make his saloon the most attractive in Sundown. There were two big mirrors behind the bar, and the shelves between them were lined with bottles of different sizes. Over them hung a portrait of a woman clothed only in a kind of sheer drapery that covered her breasts and hips.

There was nothing like that in any of Anders' saloons, but a lot of people went to them because they thought they owed Anders for taking them in, even though he charged plenty for his protection, as Briles well knew.

Since Sundown was known as a lawless town, it attracted all kinds of people. Many of them, like Briles, were there because they had no place else to go, at least for the present. Others came to sample the free life of an open town. The latter made up most of Briles' customers. He wanted more of them. He wanted the whole damn town.

Another attraction he provided for his customers was the Professor, an old man who played piano. Anders couldn't find anybody to play in his places since he killed the last piano player he'd had.

The Professor was called that because of the little glasses that perched on the end of his nose. He wasn't much of a piano player, but that was all right. He played well enough for the kind of clientele Briles attracted. He was paid in drinks, and Briles even limited those.

Briles looked up and saw Whit Anders push through the bat-wing doors. Briles could tell immediately that Anders was angry. It was easy to read Anders' moods. Everything showed on his face. Briles thought he'd be a terrible cardplayer, but Anders was too smart to play cards.

Briles, on the other hand, liked gambling. He made a little money by sitting in on poker games now and then, and he enjoyed taking a turn behind the faro layout occasionally. He wasn't gambling tonight, however, and he watched through half-closed eyes as Anders walked toward him.

"Watch him," Briles said to Grunt, who was standing behind him, leaning against the wall.

"He don't have Snake and Possum with him," Grunt said.

"They're with him," Briles said. "You might not see them, but they're with him. Right outside, I'd guess."

"Yeah. What you reckon's put the wind up his ass?"

"I don't have any idea," Briles said. "Could be anything."

By then Anders had reached the table. Briles wished him a good evening.

Anders didn't respond, and he didn't wait for an invitation to sit. He pulled back a chair and sat down.

"I'm looking for a woman," he said.

"So are a lot of these men in here," Briles told him. "It's not my fault you won't let me keep any here for them to enjoy."

That was just another reason that Briles hated Anders, who didn't mind if there was a competing saloon, just as long as there weren't any whores in it. Anders pretty much controlled that business in Sundown. Even the independent houses, like the one run by Slash, paid Anders a percentage.

"Don't be a turd, Briles," Anders said. "You know what I mean."

As a matter of fact, Briles thought he did know, in spite of what he'd told Grunt, but he wasn't going to let Anders know he'd heard about the woman who'd escaped him.

"I'm sorry, Anders," Briles said. "I don't have any idea what you're talking about."

"The hell you say." Anders looked up at Grunt, who gave him back a blank stare. "Well, maybe you don't, but you might as well know that I don't trust you, Briles."

That, Briles thought, wouldn't have been news to anybody who'd been in Sundown for more than a half hour.

"I'm sorry to hear it," he said. "I thought we were friends."

"You're a lying sack of shit."

Briles was careful not to shift in his chair or make any kind of movement at all. Anders was trying to goad him, and if Briles showed any sign of responding, Anders would probably kill him.

It was odd, but Anders had a kind of code of honor.

70

He wouldn't walk right into a man's place of business and kill him outright, and he wouldn't kill a man who was paying him for sanctuary, not unless he had a good excuse to do it. Briles didn't plan to give him one.

"I've never lied to you, Anders," he said.

"That's another one."

"I really wish you wouldn't talk that way. I'm just a businessman trying to make a little money here. I have nothing against you."

"You'd kill me in a minute if you thought you could get away with it. You don't like me, and you'd like to take over this town."

"I wouldn't know what to do with it if I had it."

"That's the damn truth, and you'll never get the chance to find out. As soon as you got rid of me, Snake and Possum would cut you to pieces."

"And where are those delightful young men?" Briles said. "I heard they were back in town and took a leading part in today's festivities."

"Festivities, my ass. That bunch of idiots came to get the woman I'm looking for, and we took care of 'em. All of 'em are dead now. You might could find yourself a little lesson in that."

"Believe me, I do. But I still don't know what woman you're referring to."

Anders stood up. "Maybe you're telling the truth. You don't look scared enough not to be. If I don't find her, I'll be back, though. Then you'd better be worried."

"I'll try to prepare myself."

"You won't need any preparations for what's gonna happen to you," Anders said.

Then he stood up and left the saloon.

"I should've shot him in the back," Grunt said when Anders had shoved through the doors.

"If you'd done that, Snake and Possum would've come in here and killed every one of us. Are you a betting man, Grunt?"

"Not so's you could tell it."

"That's too bad. If you were, I'd bet you a thousand dollars that Snake has that sawed-off shotgun of his. Have you ever seen what one of those can do in a crowded room?"

"Nope, and I don't want to," Grunt said.

"I feel the same way. Now I think I'll take a walk around town. Maybe I can find out something about that woman he was talking about."

"You want me to go with you?"

"No. You stay here and keep an eye on things. I'll be back before long."

"Yeah. If Snake and Possum don't decide to do away with you."

"They have other things to worry about tonight," Briles said. "Still, if I'm not back in a few hours, you can assume I won't be returning. You know what to do, don't you?"

"Burn this place to the ground and get out of town."

"Yes," Briles said. "That will do if you can't think of anything worse."

13

Briles hadn't gone far before he saw Anders leading a group of men to Slash Odom's place. Snake and Possum were right behind Anders, and there were five or six others. Snake was carrying the sawed-off.

Briles knew he should go back to his saloon, sit down, and have a drink. What happened to Slash was no business of his. His curiosity was too much for him, however, and he ambled on down the street to see what was going on. He stayed in the shadows and stopped about thirty yards away, close enough to see and hear what was going on.

Slash met Anders at the doorway, backlit, her hands on her hips.

"You've been here once tonight, Whit," she said. "You're welcome to come back, too, but you can't bring all your friends with you. I don't have enough girls to take care of the lot of you."

"We're not here for the girls," Anders said.

"That's all I have. If you haven't come for that, you need to go on back where you came from."

Anders stood his ground. "I'm here to look for my woman."

"I told you she wasn't here."

"Yeah, and so did everybody else I asked. Nobody will admit to seeing her, so I'm going to search every place in town until I find her. Starting right here."

"You're not coming in my place," Slash said. "You might run this town, but you don't run this house. I say who comes and goes here, not you."

"That's big talk coming from you. You know what I can do about it."

Slash's hand went to the scar on her face. Briles had heard the stories about Slash and Anders. She was the only woman who'd ever walked out on him and lived to tell about it, but she had the mark on her face to prove that it hadn't been easy.

From what Briles had been told, the scar on her face wasn't the only one she had. Anders had supposedly cut her more than once. Nobody could say for sure because, since she left Anders, she hadn't let anybody else see her body. She ran a whorehouse, but she didn't whore out herself.

"You're not going to do anything without my say-so," Slash told Anders. "Not at this house."

"I'm tired of arguing with you," Anders said. "Come here, Snake."

Snake stepped forward, separating himself from the group of men behind Anders. The barrel of the sawed-off rested in the crook of his arm.

"Either I'm coming in," Anders said, "or Snake is. And you know what he'll do when he gets inside."

"You're not scaring me, Whit. Send him in."

Anders stepped aside. He said, "You know what to do, Snake."

Snake grinned and nodded. He pointed the shotgun at Slash, who moved outside out of his way. He stepped up on the boardwalk and went through the doorway.

Briles expected to hear the roar of the shotgun, but he didn't. Not at first. Instead he saw a blur of movement, heard a thwack, and saw Snake fall to the floor.

The shotgun boomed as he fell. Briles hoped none of Slash's girls had been in the way of it.

Slash darted through the doorway and grabbed the shotgun from Snake's hands as he lay on the floor.

Snake probably didn't mind, Briles thought. He didn't even move.

Slash came back outside, holding the shotgun. Big Tits Ella stood beside her. She held a short wooden club in her hand, and Briles smiled. That explained what had happened to Snake, who was going to be madder than an agitated rattler when he woke up. *If* he woke. Big Tits Ella had hit him hard.

"Now," Slash said, looking at Anders and holding the shotgun rock steady, "you can come in. Just you. Nobody else. I'll go along with you to see that nobody gets disturbed. Not that they haven't been disturbed enough already. You're going to have to pay me for the damages."

Briles could tell that Anders didn't like the situation, but it was Possum who was most upset. He was practically jumping out of his skin. Briles thought Possum might draw his pistol, and he hoped that he would. Slash would pull the trigger of the shotgun, and that would be the end of Anders. Life in Sundown would take a sudden change for the better for Briles.

Not for Slash, though. Possum would kill her in an instant.

Anders must have known what was going through Possum's mind. He turned to him and said, "Don't touch that pistol. You stay here with the men."

"He'd better behave himself," Slash said. "If he acts up, I'm going to cut you in half with this thing."

Anders didn't have anything to say to that. He stepped up on the boardwalk, and Slash moved aside, motioning for him to precede her into the house.

Katrina stood in the alley behind the house with Lou. The night air was cool, and Katrina was still in her chemise.

"How long will we be out here?" she asked.

"Keep your voice down," Lou whispered. "We'll be here till Anders gets through looking for you."

"What if he comes out here?"

"He won't. He'll check the rooms, every one of 'em, even if there's business going on. That won't bother Anders. He won't think to come out here, though, so stop worrying."

Katrina wasn't so sure. "What if he does?"

Lou shrugged. "If he does, you better run like hell. Or you can go with him. I don't really give a goddamn. I don't see why Slash took you in, anyway. It's not like her to do it."

Katrina wrapped her arms around herself. She wondered the same thing. If Slash wanted to make her a whore, she could try, but Katrina wasn't going to cooperate. She didn't see that as being any better than what Anders would do with her.

"Maybe she's getting back at Anders," Katrina said.

"Could be. Like I said, I don't care."

"What will Anders do when he can't find me?"

"How the hell would I know? He might burn the place down. Probably would if he wasn't making money from it. He'll just go look everyplace else he can think of. Then he'll go back to his saloon and try to figure out what the hell happened to you."

"Won't he know I'm here in town somewhere?"

"Maybe. Or he might think somebody smuggled you out. Either way, he won't be happy. That'll keep things stirred up for a while."

Katrina didn't care if things were stirred up. All she cared about was getting away. She might have tried running from Lou, but Lou had a derringer in her right hand, and she looked like someone who knew how to use it.

Katrina sighed, and her shoulders slumped. But only for a moment. She didn't know how she could escape, but she wasn't going to give up. Not until she'd gotten away or was dead. Right now the second seemed a lot more likely than the first, but even that would be better than letting Anders get his hands on her. She promised herself she'd never let that happen, no matter what.

"Satisfied?" Slash asked when Anders had finished searching the house.

Anders clearly wasn't. He was mad, and he was puzzled.

"I thought for sure you had her," he said.

"You've looked in every room. She's not here. Now will you leave me alone?"

Anders gave her an appraising look. "I wish I trusted you, Slash."

"You don't trust anybody, Whit. It's one of your less lovable qualities."

"I trusted you once. Maybe that's how I learned my lesson."

76

"I don't care how you learned it. I just want you out of my house. Now."

She motioned toward him with the shotgun, and he moved down the hallway. They walked down the stairs. Snake was sitting on one of the parlor couches. Ella was attending to his head.

"Hardly even scratched him," she said. "Gonna have a big old knot, though."

"You owe me a poke for that," Snake told her. "On the house."

"Sure, honey, I'd love it. You'll have to ask Slash about the 'on the house' part, though."

"It's a deal," Slash said. "You come back when you're feeling better. Don't bring your shotgun."

She broke it open and took out the cartridges. Then she handed the shotgun to Anders. She kept the cartridges.

"Let's go," Anders said to Snake.

"Where to?" Snake asked, rising a little shakily.

"Briles' saloon. If the woman's not here, she's there. Has to be."

"What if she got out of town?"

"Shut up," Anders said. "Get your ass out of here."

Snake wobbled out the door, and Anders followed. Slash watched them go with a smile.

When the gang of men was well clear of the house, she sent Ella out back to get Katrina and Lou. It was time to do some more thinking about how to use the girl to get back at Anders. Slash knew she'd come up with something, sooner or later.

14 ⸺ •

Fargo slipped away from Marian eventually and went to Buck's place for the rest of the night. The company wasn't as pleasant, and there was no bed to sleep on. Besides that, when Buck snored he sounded like a hog rooting around in the bottom of a trough for the last of the slop.

Fargo rolled out a pallet on the floor and made the best of it, however. He needed a few hours' rest before getting ready for his return trip to Sundown.

Early the next morning Fargo awoke to the sound and smell of bacon sizzling in the pan. Buck might not have much grub, but what he had was just fine with Fargo.

"You're gonna get yourself killed, is what you're gonna do," Buck said as they ate.

"Now who's the bundle of sunshine?" Fargo said.

Buck had made biscuits, and while they weren't exactly floating off the table, Fargo had eaten worse. He took another one.

"You said yourself Snake and Possum know you," Buck reminded him. "They'd carve you up and take your guts for garters. They'd have fun doing it, too."

"Not if I don't look like myself."

Buck appraised him for a few seconds. "I don't know anybody else around that's big as you. Be mighty hard to fool 'em."

"I didn't say it would be easy. I've thought of a way that might work, though."

Buck arched his bushy eyebrows. "You have? Well, you gonna tell me what it is or make me guess?"

"I'll need your help," Fargo said, chewing on his biscuit, "so I'll have to tell you."

"Well? Let's have it. I'm waitin'."

"I'm going to be you," Fargo said.

"Me? Now I know you're crazy. Have you taken a good look at me? I'm a foot shorter than you, and I'm a good sight older. I'm kinda on the scrawny side, and you're like a slab of rock. But that's not the biggest problem."

"What is, then?"

"I'm mighty damn handsome, but you're a little on the homely side."

"Yeah," Fargo said. "But there's not much I can do about that. There's something else, too. You have something I need."

"Besides my looks, you mean?"

"Yeah, besides that. I need a mount."

"You can rent yourself that pinto. That's a mighty fine animal."

"A mighty fine animal's not what you'd be riding if you went to Sundown, though."

"Aw, Fargo, you ain't askin' for what I think you are. Are you?"

"I probably am. I want to ride Agnes."

"Damn," Buck said.

Fargo's plan didn't involve becoming Buck but instead becoming someone like him: an old miner, maybe, come to Fort Benton on the way to the gold strikes and looking for a little fun before heading out to work a claim. Or an old man who'd lived in the mountains for years, clinging to the old ways, trapping and hunting for a living.

"You might not be as handsome as me, but you don't look old," Buck pointed out, looking at Fargo's mane of black hair and his thick black beard.

"We'll have to do something about that," Fargo said.

"Like what?"

"First of all you'll have to cut my hair."

"I ain't a barber. I ain't got nothing but a bowie knife to use on you."

"That'll do," Fargo said. "Let's get started."

After Buck had hacked off most of Fargo's hair, Fargo went to work on his beard, reducing it to stubble. Then he mixed up some of Buck's biscuit flour with a little bacon grease and spread it through what was left of his hair, leaving it streaked with gray. Then he rubbed the mixture in the bristles on his face.

"You look passable old," Buck said. "You might get by better'n I thought you would. What're you gonna do about them clothes, though?"

Fargo knew his buckskins wouldn't do. They weren't right for an old prospector. They might pass muster if he posed as a trapper, and if they'd had more hard use. They hadn't, however, so Fargo gave Buck some money and asked him to go out and find him something to wear.

"Be sure whatever you get is well used. I don't care how bad it looks."

"You makin' a comment about my duds?" Buck said.

"Wouldn't even consider it. Not that you couldn't stand a little cleaning up."

Buck ignored that. "What're you plannin' to do while I'm gone?"

"I'll practice stooping," Fargo said. "And bring Agnes back with you."

"I was hopin' you'd forget about Agnes."

"Not a chance. She's an important part of the disguise."

"You better bring her back here, Fargo. I ain't got much, just this shack and that mule."

It seemed like everybody wanted promises from him, Fargo thought.

"I'll bring her back," he said. "You don't have to worry about that."

"I do worry, though. About you and Agnes both. I'm not sure you know just what you're walkin' into. That Anders is one tough son of a bitch."

"So am I," Fargo said.

By the time Buck returned, Fargo had been working on his impersonation for almost an hour. However, he didn't want to give Buck a sample until after he'd changed clothes.

"Got those from a fella who was down on his luck,"

Buck said about the clothes, which included a pair of denim pants with ground-in dirt and holes in the knees, a shirt that had possibly never been washed, and a pair of worn boots. "Couldn't find nothin' else that would come near to fittin' you."

The clothes, while smelly, almost fit. If anything, they were a little loose, which Fargo preferred. The boots were a little bit too big, but that was fine, too. Fargo slipped his Arkansas toothpick into the right one, where it rested comfortably. He didn't think anyone would look for it there.

"What about your pistol?" Buck said. "You're likely to need it, not that it's gonna save you."

"I'll carry it in my pack."

"What pack?" Buck said.

"The one I'm borrowing from you. Doesn't have to be a good one."

"First my mule, and now my pack," Buck grumbled. "Seems like I might as well go with you since you're takin' just about ever'thing I own."

"You can go if you want to," Fargo said, "but I wouldn't advise it."

"Didn't say I was goin'. Said I might as well. Let me get that pack for you."

"What about Agnes?"

"She's right outside." Buck rummaged around under his cot and brought out the pack. It was worn and ragged. He held it up for Fargo to admire. "Ain't got nothin' in it. Fill it up with whatever you please."

Fargo took the pack and stashed his pistol in it. He didn't think anyone would look for it there. He planned to pick up a few more items that might come in handy on his way out of town.

"I just need one more thing," Fargo said.

"Don't look at me," Buck said. "You got ever'thing I own already."

"Not quite."

Fargo snatched off Buck's hat and put it on his own head.

"Damnation," Buck said, smoothing down the white wisps of hair on top of his head. "You can't have that hat. It's the only one I got."

It didn't fit anyway, and Fargo wanted something he could pull down low over his face.

"Go out and see if you can find me one," Fargo said, tossing the hat back to Buck.

"A man's not gonna give up his hat."

"Somebody who needs a drink bad enough will. I want a beat-up hat."

Buck said he'd see what he could do, and in a short while he was back with just the hat Fargo wanted. It was black and dusty, dented and worn, with a wide brim that hid Fargo's face when he pulled the hat down. It also concealed most of his hair, which would be an advantage if the mixture Fargo had put on it to make it look gray failed to last.

"You look older since I left," Buck said.

Fargo had dirtied up his face a little and put a few lines on it with grease and charcoal.

"I reckon I'm aging fast," Fargo told him.

"Damnation," Buck said in surprise. "Now you even sound old. Older than I do, by God."

Fargo had been working on the voice, and he was glad to hear that it passed muster with Buck.

"How about this?" Fargo said, walking across the room toward the door.

Buck watched him with a critical eye. "I hope you don't think I crip around like that."

"You walk like a younker. I don't want to look like I'm as spry as you. Snake and Possum might spot me."

"You ain't lookin' spry, for sure. If you don't slip up, you might get away with it for a few hours."

"I think it's going to take me longer than that to get anything done. I don't know where Anders has the girl. I don't even know what she looks like."

"Then you better pray for luck. Might pray that Snake and Possum ain't even there, while you're at it."

"I can't count on luck," Fargo said. "Tell me what Katrina looks like."

"Mighty pretty. Black hair and blue eyes. She was wearin' a weddin' dress when Anders grabbed her and carried her off."

Fargo figured he didn't need to worry about the dress. Anders would have had her out of that soon enough. It was what else Anders might have done that worried Fargo.

"They'll be buryin' Nick tomorrow," Buck said. "You think you'll be back for that?"

"Don't count on it," Fargo told him.

"It'd be good if Katrina could be here for it."

"It'll be good if I get her out of Sundown at all."

"When you plan to go after her?"

"Right now's as good a time as any. You got a saddle on Agnes?"

"Yeah. You treat that mule right, Fargo, you hear me?"

"I hear you," Fargo said.

15

Sundown didn't look any better than it had the first time Fargo had seen it, and the closer he got, the worse it looked.

The vultures didn't help a bit. Fargo saw them before he saw the town. They floated lazily in a blue sky, circling down lower and lower for whatever it was that interested them in the road ahead.

When Fargo got nearer, he saw what they were after. There was a body hanging up against the fence on one side of the road. Several vultures sat on the fence, while a couple perched on the body. One was on the head, and another was on a shoulder, pulling at the face with its beak.

It had to be Stuver that they were having fun with, Fargo thought. When he passed by he could smell the decaying flesh, but there wasn't enough left of the body's face to be recognized. It was Stuver, though. The sheriff's badge was still pinned to his shirt.

Welcome to Sundown, Fargo thought.

He rode Agnes on into town. Several people saw him, and he heard a few jibes about his mount and appearance. He didn't let them bother him. He rode up to a water trough and got down to let the mule take a drink. He made sure to look as if he were stiff and sore from his ride.

Agnes drank noisily. When she was finished, Fargo led her to a hitch rail in front of a saloon. He looped the reins around the rail and gave the town a good look.

There wasn't much to it, just the one long main street, lined with buildings that appeared to be mostly saloons, whorehouses, and hotels. A couple of stores and a livery stable were located at the end of the street. There were no houses at all, but Fargo wasn't surprised. Most people in Sundown weren't looking to settle there. They'd be moving on when they thought the time was right or when they believed the law wasn't looking for them anymore.

"What're you looking at, you old fart?"

It took Fargo a second to realize the man was talking to him.

"Wasn't looking at anything," he said, but now he turned his eyes to the man, keeping his head down so that it would be shadowed by the hat brim.

The man was tall and wide. He had a mean look about him, but then Fargo figured everybody in Sundown looked like that. Another man, smaller but just as mean-looking, stood beside him. They laughed at Fargo. The smaller one said, "He's wondering who we are, Trask. You want to tell him?"

"Hell, no, Zack. You can tell him. Maybe he'll get right back on that sorry-assed mule of his and ride out of here."

"I'll thank you not to talk that way about Agnes," Fargo said.

"Agnes?" Trask said. "What the hell kind of a name is that?"

"It's Agnes' name," Fargo said.

He started to step up on the boardwalk, but Trask put up a hand to stop him.

"You ain't heard who we are, yet," Trask said. "Tell him, Zack."

"We're the Coleman brothers. Maybe you've heard of us."

"Can't say as I have," Fargo said.

That wasn't true. Fargo had heard of them all right. They were wanted for murder and rape in California and a couple of other states.

Zack said, "You right sure you never heard of us?"

"Don't think so. Might have, though. I'm a little forgetful lately. Sometimes I can't even remember Agnes' name."

Fargo stepped up on the boardwalk, and this time the Colemans didn't try to stop him.

"Can a man get a drink in here?" Fargo said, indicating the building.

"Sure, if he's got the money. It's a saloon."

"I was wondering about the kind of welcome I might get," Fargo said, "because of what I saw on the way into town. Gave me the idea that this might not be a very hospitable place."

Trask laughed. "You mean the lawman?"

"I guess he was, once," Fargo said. "All he looked like to me was dead."

"He's dead because he came after Whit Anders. You ain't gonna try to say you never heard of him, are you?"

"I know who he is. Runs this town, is what they say."

"This is his saloon. And speaking of the kind of welcome you'd get, I'm not so sure he wants any old galoots like you coming in there. He ain't in a good mood today. He might kick your ass out."

Fargo wondered what had upset Anders. After abducting Katrina and killing a sheriff, Anders should have been feeling fine. Maybe Fargo could find out something when he went inside.

"I sure could use a drink," he said. "I guess I'll just have to chance it."

"Well, then," Zack said, "you just go right on in."

Fargo pushed open the bat-wing doors and was about to go inside the saloon when Trask put a hand in the middle of his back and gave him a hard shove.

Fargo wasn't caught off guard as much as an old man would have been, but he pretended he was. He stumbled across the room, windmilling his arms. He veered sharply to his left, and it appeared that he was going to plow right into the bar. At the last second he brought himself to a stop. He teetered on his legs as if deciding which way to fall, waving his arms in what seemed to be an attempt to balance himself.

Trask and Zack walked into the saloon, smiling at the general laughter that had greeted Fargo's undignified entrance. The two men went straight to Fargo. It was plain that they weren't through having their fun with him.

Or so they thought.

Zack got to him first. Fargo half turned and swung his

arms wildly. He hit Zack in the face, first with his right hand and then with his left, palms open. Zack fell back against the bar with an astonished look on his face, which was now crimson on both sides from the slaps.

"Shit!" Fargo said. "I'm sorry, Mr. Coleman."

As he said it, Fargo stumbled forward and careened right into Trask, butting him in the chest with his head and sending him falling to the floor on his ass.

Fargo reeled to the side. "Damn! I'm sorry, Mr. Coleman. Somebody help me! I can't get my balance!"

He lurched from one side of the saloon to the other. When he came to the bar, he somehow got an elbow into Zack's stomach. Zack folded in the middle and hit the floor, just as Fargo kicked over a spittoon, dumping its contents near Zack's face.

Trask was about to get to his feet as Fargo staggered back in his direction. Trask saw what was about to happen and put his hands up in front of his face, but they weren't strong enough to stop Fargo's dancing foot, which kicked them back and into Trask's nose.

Trask fell back down, blood leaking between his fingers.

"Somebody kill that son of a bitch!" Zack yelled, pushing himself up. Something brownish-yellow and slick dripped off his face.

"I'm sorry! I'm sorry!" Fargo said. "I didn't mean any harm to you fellas."

He dropped into a chair and held onto a table as if to stop his St. Vitus' dance. The table hopped up and down twice, thunking against the floor, and then it stopped.

"I think I'm all right now," Fargo said. "I get all discombobulated when I'm off balance. My head spins and I can't hardly see. Did anybody get a look at who pushed me? That's who's to blame. Not me. I couldn't help it. I just came in here for a drink."

Trask and Zack were both on their feet now. Trask looked at his bloody hands and pulled a bandanna from his pocket. He wiped his face and then his hands. Zack wiped his face, too. What was on there was less pleasant even than blood.

"We're gonna slit your goddamn gizzle," Zack told Fargo. "Just as soon as we get cleaned up."

Fargo looked around, a pitiful, pleading old man. He spread his hands in supplication.

"Can't somebody tell these two fellas that it wasn't my fault? I just came in for a drink and somebody pushed me. I can't help it if I get all wild and wiggly when I can't get my balance."

A big man wearing a plaid shirt stood up. He had a slight grin on his face, as if he hadn't been too displeased by what he'd just seen.

"You say you came in here for a drink?"

"That's right. I can pay for it, too."

"My name's Anders," the man said. "I own this place. You gave me the first laugh I've had today, so I'll buy your drink. Trask, you and Zack leave him alone. It was just an accident." He paused and gave Trask a meaningful look. "Somebody pushed him."

"Goddamn it," Trask said.

"That's enough, Trask. I'll stand drinks for you and Zack, too. Hell, I'll just buy a round for the house."

A cheer went up as everyone stampeded toward the bar. A couple of men stopped to pat Fargo on the back and thanked him for getting them a free drink.

"Glad to do it," Fargo said. "But like I said, I didn't mean to do anything. I'm sure sorry I hurt those two gentlemen."

"Those aren't gentlemen," somebody said. "That's the Coleman boys. They don't take kindly to gettin' whipped. I'd watch out for 'em if I was you."

Fargo knew he'd made a couple of enemies, but he didn't intend to be pushed around, even if he was supposed to be old and clumsy. The Coleman brothers had picked on the wrong galoot.

Anders brought Fargo's drink over to the table and set it in front of him.

"Thanks," Fargo said. "I do appreciate it."

"What's your name?" Anders said. His momentary good mood seemed to have deserted him.

"Luke," Fargo said. "Luke Scott." He took a sip of his drink. "Smooth," he lied.

"I never heard of you," Anders said.

"Well, now that's not surprising. I haven't ever been here before. I heard of you, though. Heard about how if a fella wanted a drink or a woman, this here town was the place to come. So here I am."

"Where'd you come from?"

"Been around here for years, doing some trapping up in the mountains. Heard about the big gold strike and thought I might try my hand at panning since the trapping's about played out, but first I wanted to get a little whiskey in me. And find that woman I was talking about."

Fargo took another sip, while Anders hooked a chair with his foot and pulled it to him. He sat down and gave Fargo a hard look.

"What woman is that?" he said.

"Well, just about any woman at all. When you been living like I have, off away from towns and such, you're not too particular about what she looks like."

Anders didn't look entirely convinced. "I'm looking for a woman, too," he said.

Fargo deliberately misunderstood him. He gave Anders a disappointed look and said, "You mean this town don't have any whores?"

Anders leaned back in his chair and looked around the room. Fargo had a look, too. The Coleman brothers hadn't accepted their drinks. They'd left the place. Everyone else seemed sociable enough, laughing and enjoying the free drink. Snake and Possum leaned against the back wall, watching everything that went on. Snake cradled a sawed-off shotgun.

They paid Fargo no attention, which he took to mean that his disguise was working just fine. Fargo didn't see a single woman in the saloon.

"I guess you do mean it about the whores," Fargo said, waving a hand at the room. "I don't see any."

"They're not here. This saloon's for drinking. If you want a woman, you have to go next door to Slash's place. Or any of the other houses. Hell, you can go to my other saloons. There's women there. Just not in this one."

"Well, then," Fargo said. He tossed down the rest of his drink. "If there's that many women around town, you ought to be able to find you a woman without much trouble."

"I don't want just any woman. I want one particular woman. Did you come through Fort Benton on your way here?"

"Yep," Fargo said. "Didn't stop long, though."

"Did you hear anything about a woman being taken from there?"

"Didn't stay long enough to talk to anybody. I wanted to get here and have a drink." Fargo picked up his glass. "I reckon I could stand another one."

Anders didn't offer to pay this time, so Fargo went to the bar and got a drink.

When Fargo sat back down, Anders said, "Did you meet anybody on the trail when you came to town?"

"Not a soul," Fargo said, "unless you count that sheriff hanging out there on the fence."

Anders grinned, his good humor surfacing again. "Taught that son of a bitch a lesson, him and the men that rode with him. Nobody comes into Sundown if I don't allow it. This is my town."

"Won't get any argument from me," Fargo said.

"I took a woman from Fort Benton yesterday," Anders said. "Brought her here for a little entertainment. She's gone now, though."

"Where'd she go?" Fargo asked, and took a drink.

"I don't know. I'll find her, though, you can bet on that." He stood up. "If you want a woman, try Slash's place. It's the closest."

"I'll do that," Fargo said.

Anders walked to the back of the room and said something to Snake and Possum. They laughed, and Anders went on back, presumably to his office. Snake and Possum looked out over the room, taking everything in.

Fargo ignored them and thought about his conversation with Anders. Anders had told him a little more than he'd known when he'd come into town, but not much. It appeared that Katrina had somehow escaped from Anders, but that she might still be in town somewhere. If she was, Anders would be turning up every rock until he found her, Fargo thought.

He finished his drink. Nobody was paying him any mind. Snake and Possum were talking together and not looking his way. He was just an old fart who'd provided a few minutes of entertainment and roughed up the Coleman boys by accident, and now everybody had forgotten about him.

He got up and hobbled out of the saloon. He thought he might as well see what the woman named Slash had to offer.

16

What Slash had to offer Fargo remained to be seen. What she had to offer Ken Briles was Katrina.

Slash had thought about it all night. For years she'd wanted to repay Whit Anders for what he'd done to her, and the girl seemed the best opportunity to exact some kind of recompense.

It might have been possible to smuggle Katrina out of town and frustrate Whit that way, but Slash wanted to do more than frustrate him. Her hand went to her face, and a finger traced the scar. She wanted Whit to suffer as much as she had, and the way she saw it, the only person who might be able to help her was Briles.

She sent Lou to Briles' saloon with a note. Lou went through the alleys to avoid being seen and arrived at the back door of Briles' saloon.

When she went inside, she found herself looking down the barrel of a .44.

"Just stop right there," Grunt said.

Lou said, "I'm not going anywhere. You know who I am, Grunt. Put that gun down."

Grunt didn't move. "State your business."

"I'm here to see Briles. Slash sent me."

Grunt moved back a little, and Lou followed. They were in a hallway at the back of the saloon. Briles' office was located on the left.

"I'll ask him if he wants to see you," Grunt said.

He tapped on the door of the office.

"What?" Briles said from inside.

"St. Louis Lou's here. Says Slash sent her."

"Is she armed?"

"I can't tell. Want me to search her?"

Grunt looked eager to do it, Lou thought.

"Hell, I guess we can trust Lou. Let her in."

"I'm sorry he disappointed you, big fella," Lou said when Grunt opened the door. "Come on down to Slash's for a visit, and you can search me all you want."

"Just go in," Grunt said.

Lou went into the office with a flirt of her skirt. Briles sat behind an oak desk. His eyes were puffy, and he didn't look as if he'd had much sleep. He was leaning back in his chair with his feet up on the desk, and Lou thought he might have been trying to take a nap.

A curtain was pulled over the small window, so it was dim in the room, as if the sunlight might have bothered Briles. Or maybe he just didn't want anybody outside to see him. As soon as Lou was well inside, Grunt closed the door behind her.

"You bastards are sure touchy this morning," Lou said, sitting in a chair near the desk.

"You know why," Briles said. "We had a little visit from Anders last night. It was the second one he made. The same thing happened to you."

Lou figured he meant that Anders had searched the saloon. Briles wasn't likely to take that lightly. He hated Anders already, and to have him storming around in the saloon, bothering the customers and disrupting business, would have really riled him. No wonder he hadn't gotten any sleep.

"We didn't have much trouble with him," Lou said. "Big Tits Ella pretty much took care of things."

Briles gave her a sour grin. "I heard about that. I wonder if Slash would trade me Ella for Grunt."

Lou matched his grin. "Ella could do Grunt's job just fine. I don't think he could handle hers, though."

"Probably not," Briles said. He took his feet off the desk, planted them on the floor, and leaned forward with his arms on the desk. "But you didn't come here to talk about Ella and Grunt, did you?"

"No."

Lou reached across the desk and handed him the note

Slash had given her. When she did, her breasts were exposed to good advantage. She noticed Briles admiring them.

"You haven't come around to see me lately," she said.

Briles unfolded the note. "I've been busy."

He read the note slowly, then read it over again. He laid it on the desk when he was finished.

"You know what's in this?" he asked. He tapped the note with his index finger.

"I might have an idea," Lou said, "but Slash didn't tell me."

"Slash wants me to come for a visit. Business she says. What kind of business?"

"Like I said, Slash didn't tell me."

"But you have an idea."

"Look, Briles, she's the one who wants to talk to you, and she'll tell you all about it if you come."

"She says not to let anybody see me."

"You can get there through the alley. She won't even have anybody standing at the back door to stick a gun in your face when you come in."

"She says to come now."

Lou was getting impatient. "Well, come on. I'm going back, and you can go with me."

"Where I go, Grunt goes."

"When did that start?"

"It started when Anders came in here and rousted the place last night. I never liked him, which he well knows, but we've gotten along in the past. When he came here to search this place, though, he was as much as calling me a liar. I told him I didn't have his woman here, but he didn't believe me. He was like a crazy man."

Lou looked at the curtained window. Briles caught the look.

"I'm not hiding from him," he said. "I just don't want to be shot in the back while I'm sitting at my desk."

Lou had heard enough. She stood up. "You gonna come with me or not?"

"I'm coming," Briles said. "So is Grunt."

"That's all right with me. Maybe he'll spend a little money while you're talking to Slash."

"He'll be watching for Anders."

"Ella can do that as well as he can. Maybe better."

Briles nodded. "You're right, but I want Grunt on the alert."

Lou shrugged. "You're the boss."

"Not yet," Briles said. "Maybe someday I will be."

Yeah, Lou thought. *And someday pigs will fly.*

Fargo didn't want anything from Slash's girls but information. He knew that even if he was really as old as he looked, they'd be more than happy to show him a good time as long as he had the money to pay for it, but he hadn't come to Sundown to have fun. He'd come there to find Katrina.

There was one sure thing about any whorehouse. They were good sources of information. Men came in for entertainment, and they often let their guard down in the course of what went on. All Fargo had to do was find somebody who knew something and convince her to tell him.

He went and got his pack off the mule. Then he wandered into Slash's place and stood in the parlor. He was welcomed by a blond woman with a scar on her face. Even with the scar, she didn't look bad to Fargo, and he kind of wished he could indulge himself.

"Hey, stranger," the woman said. "My name's Slash, and I run this establishment. See anything you like?"

A couple of women lounged in the room, wearing next to nothing. One of them had big breasts and a hard face. The other had black hair, black eyes, and a sweet, round face. She looked to be no more than sixteen.

"I might be interested in her," Fargo said. He set down his pack and pointed to the young one.

A disgusted look appeared on Slash's face, but it was gone so quickly that most people would have missed it. Fargo didn't. It did surprise him a little, however. He would have expected a whore to want his money, no matter what the situation was. He didn't see what difference it made that he was supposedly an old man. He was pretty sure the girl had been with plenty of men before, even if the men hadn't been old galoots like he was supposed to be.

"That's Pretty Penny," Slash said. "She's a little young, don't you think?"

"You could be right about that." Fargo pretended to consider the matter. "Maybe you'd be closer to the right age for me."

Pretty Penny laughed sharply, but Slash glared at her and the sound was cut off before it had hardly begun.

Fargo looked at her, too. "Did I say something funny?"

"You're new here, mister," Penny said. "So you don't know the rules. Slash don't go upstairs with nobody."

Fargo turned his eyes to Slash and gave her the once-over.

"Seems like a waste of talent. The more I think about it, ma'am, the more I think you'd be the right one for me."

He wasn't sure at all. He thought the youngster would be the most likely to let something slip if he asked her a few questions and then pretended to be unable to perform. However, something was going on, and Fargo wanted to know what it was. Any information he could get might be useful to him.

"You heard what Penny said," Slash told him. "I don't go upstairs with anybody."

"Can't blame you for that," Fargo said. "I don't like to go upstairs, myself. My old knees get kind of creaky if I have to climb. I can come down a stair all right, but going up is mighty rough. Maybe you have a room down here we could use."

Penny laughed again, and so did the other woman.

"What did I say?" Fargo asked.

"Nobody goes in Slash's room," Penny said. "Not even us girls."

"I'd sure admire to do it, though," Fargo said to Slash. "I wouldn't have to climb the stairs, and I do believe you're the best-looking woman in this place."

The other two women didn't like hearing that, but Fargo didn't care. If a little flattery would get him what he wanted, he'd be happy to use it.

Fargo was pretty sure Slash was weakening, maybe even considering letting him into her room, when there was a knock at the door to the back of the house.

"You go upstairs with Penny," Slash said. "She'll show you a good time."

Fargo was going to protest that his knees wouldn't make the trip, but Slash turned and left the room.

Penny stood up. "Come along, old man," she said. "I'm gonna make you feel young again."

"I'll bet you can do that," Fargo said. "I just hope my old knees don't give out before we get up to the top of those stairs."

"You wouldn't want to miss what'll be waiting for you up there." Penny took his hand. "I'll help you."

Fargo took his pack and went up the stairs with her, complaining about his knees all the way.

17

When they got to Penny's room, the girl took Fargo inside. She told him to sit in a straight-backed wooden chair while she undressed.

"I don't think you have to do that," Fargo said. He set his pack down by the chair. "I'm too old and tired for a young filly like you."

Penny gave him what she must have thought of as a seductive smile.

"You don't really think Slash is prettier than I am, do you?"

"Nope, but she's a lot closer to my age."

"You don't have to worry about your age. You just wait till I start taking off my clothes. You'll start to feel eighteen again."

"You don't have on enough clothes to take off any," Fargo said. "And I don't want to feel eighteen again. I just want to talk a while."

Penny stared at him as if he might have lost his mind. Maybe she'd never heard that from a man before.

"It'll cost you just as much," she said.

"I don't care about that," Fargo told her. "Why don't you humor an old man? Let me talk a while, and we can be friends."

A shrewd looked came into Penny's eyes. "Money first, talk later."

"Usually a fella pays after."

"Usually a fella doesn't just want to talk. Pay or get out."

Fargo admired her business acumen. He gave her ten

dollars, which he figured was more than she'd ever gotten for a poke in her short life.

Penny took the money and put it in the drawer of the washstand. Then she sat on the bed, crossed her legs to give Fargo a little show of what he was missing, and said, "What do you want to talk about?"

"Just anything. When a man's been out in the mountains as long as I have, it's a treat just to listen to a pretty woman's voice."

"I'm not gonna tell you my sad life story, if that's what you want to hear. I'm a whore because that's what I want to be. Nobody forced me into it or anything like that."

"Tell me about Slash, then," Fargo said. "Bound to be a good story about a woman like that."

"You mean the scar?"

"Yeah, the scar. How'd she come by it?"

"Whit Anders gave it to her." Penny looked thoughtful. "That's why she doesn't let anybody go with her. Not just that scar. They say there's others. In other places."

Now that was what Fargo considered interesting news. Slash was one person in Sundown who'd have reason not to care for Whit Anders, and Fargo wished more than ever that he'd been able to get her off to herself for some talking.

"Why'd Anders do it?" he asked.

"She worked for him in the saloon next door, but she got tired of the way he treated her and the girls. She saved up some money he didn't know about and left." Penny paused. "He caught her before she got very far and brought her back. When she got back, she had the scars. I guess they were fresh then. Anyway, that's why there's no girls in that saloon. Anders has never let any other women work there. He finds his own women somewhere else. Slash runs this house, and she's never tried to leave again."

While she talked, Penny let her fingers play with the hem of her chemise. She had tugged it up almost to the top of her hips. She looked down at herself and smiled at Fargo.

"You tired of talking yet?"

"Not yet. I was just over in Anders' saloon, and he was mighty mad. Something about a woman he'd lost. Must have been one he found somewhere else, like you said. You know how he lost her? Sounds like it would make a good story."

Penny pulled down the hem of the chemise. Fargo could tell she was flustered.

"I don't know anything about that," she said, but it was clear to Fargo that she was lying.

"He said he'd looked everywhere for her," Fargo said. "Didn't he come here?"

"Well, yeah, maybe he did. Big Tits Ella, that's her you saw down in the parlor, she hit Snake with her club. Anders came in here and looked all around, but he didn't find anybody."

Penny kept her eyes down and didn't look at Fargo while she spoke. He figured that she knew a lot more than she was telling him.

"Who's Snake?" Fargo said, pretending that he didn't know.

"He's one of Anders' bodyguards. Mean as hell." Penny hugged herself as if she knew something about Snake from personal experience. "Snake didn't like it when he got hit."

Fargo figured that was an understatement. Considering the way Snake had tried to get back at him, Big Tits Ella had better be watching her back.

Fargo heard talking in the hall. Another customer, he figured. A door opened somewhere, and there was more talking, all of it in low voices. After a few seconds, several people walked by the door.

Penny ignored the sounds and fussed with her chemise, avoiding Fargo's gaze. The footsteps passed, and all was quiet outside again.

"What would've happened if Anders had found that woman here?" Fargo said.

Penny hugged herself again, tighter this time.

"He'd probably have killed somebody."

"Not you, though," Fargo said.

"Not me, not unless I got in his way. He'd kill anybody that got in his way." Penny paused, then added quickly, "He didn't find her, though, because she's not here. Let's talk about something else."

Her fingers fidgeted with the hem of the chemise. The more she lied, Fargo thought, the more nervous she got. He was glad now that he'd gotten to talk to her instead of Slash, who would never have been so easy to see through.

"I'm glad that woman's not here," Fargo said. "That Anders sounds like a tough character, not anybody I'd want to tangle with. I saw a sheriff hanging against a wall when I came into town. Anders says that was his doing."

"It was, and he'd do it to anybody who crossed him. Or maybe he'd scar them up, like he did Slash. Are you sure you don't want me to get undressed?"

"I'm having a fine time just the way we are," Fargo said.

"Well, I'm not. If you're not going to give me a poke or even look at me, you might as well just leave. I'm tired of all this talking."

Fargo tried to cajole her into saying more, but Penny wasn't going to be persuaded. She lay back on the bed, her head on the pillow, and closed her eyes. She lay very still.

Fargo said a couple of things to her, but he might as well have been talking to a statue. He gave it up, took his pack, and went out of the room. Penny didn't even open her eyes to see him leave.

When Fargo got back to the parlor, Big Tits Ella was gone. A redhead sat in a chair reading a book. Fargo didn't think it was the Bible. She put the book down when she saw Fargo.

"My name's St. Louis Lou," she said, giving him a businesslike smile. "Did you have a good time?"

"Sure did," Fargo told her and started for the back exit.

"Hold on," Lou said. "You can't go out that way."

"I need to talk to Slash. I won't bother her any."

Lou stood up and put herself in Fargo's path.

"You won't bother her any because you're not going back that way."

Fargo took another step.

"Ella!" Lou called, and from somewhere Ella appeared with her club in her hand.

"There's no call for that," Fargo said, but he was too late. Ella was already swinging at his head.

Fargo dropped his pack and put up a hand. The club smacked into his palm, and he closed his grip. Ella tried to jerk her club away from him, but he held on tight. He snapped his arm back, and the club came out of Ella's grasp.

"Goddamn," Ella said. "You're mighty strong for such an old coot. Mighty quick, too."

Fargo was getting tired of being called names just because he looked old. An old man ought not to have to put up with such disrespect. He jabbed the club in the direction of Ella's face, and she backed away.

"I'm going to talk to Slash now," he said. "St. Louis Lou can read you something from the Bible."

"That's not the Bible," Lou said.

"I didn't think it was," Fargo said.

He bent over and grabbed hold of his pack.

"You gonna let me have my club back?" Ella asked him.

"Maybe later," he said.

As he left the parlor, he heard Ella say, "I don't think that son of a bitch is as old as he looks."

Fargo didn't bother to knock on Slash's door. He pushed it open and went right into her private room, which was quite a bit different from what Fargo had seen of the house so far. There were a divan, a fancy canopy bed, a chest of drawers, a writing desk, a modesty screen, and a washstand. Fargo would have expected to see a mirror on the wall of a fancy room like that, but there wasn't one. He guessed he knew why.

Fargo closed the door. Slash sat at the little writing desk. She turned to look at Fargo when he entered.

"I wondered who would be so rude as to barge in," she said. "I knew it wouldn't be one of the girls."

Fargo tossed Ella's club on the bed. "They didn't want me to come. They tried to stop me."

Slash looked at the club and then back at Fargo.

"You took that away from Ella?"

She sounded surprised. Fargo just nodded.

"You weren't satisfied with Penny?" she said. "Is that why you're here?"

"Nope," Fargo said, his voice changing slightly. "I'm here about another woman."

"You're not as old as you look," Slash said, catching the change in his tone. "Are you."

It wasn't a question, but Fargo decided he'd answer.

"Hard to say. I don't know how old I look."

"What did you say your name was?"

"I don't think I said. I'm calling myself Scott. Luke Scott."

"That's not your name, though."

"No." Fargo decided to tell her the truth. He didn't think he had any reason not to. "My name's Fargo. I want to talk to you about a woman named Katrina. I came to take her back to Fort Benton."

18

"I saw 'em, I tell you," Snake said. "It was Briles and that redheaded one that they call St. Louis Lou, going in the back door."

Snake had been out to the privy, and on his way there he'd seen Briles and Lou as they went into Slash's place. He'd had urgent business in the privy, maybe because of something he'd eaten, so he couldn't take the time to go back inside until he'd finished. It took him longer than usual, but when he was done, he felt a lot better.

"You sure it was them?" Possum said when Snake told him who he'd seen.

"Damn right I'm sure." Snake got a reminiscent look. "That Lou's about the only redhead in town. Natural, too, I'm here to tell you. I couldn't miss her."

"We better tell Anders."

"He said he didn't want to be bothered."

"The hell with that. He'll want to hear about it if Briles and Slash are getting together."

Possum was right. Anders was a little upset at first, since he'd had no more sleep than Briles the previous night. He'd been taking a rest on his office divan, but when he heard what Snake had to say, he was instantly awake.

"Where's your shotgun?" Anders asked Snake as he pulled on his boots.

"I left it with the bartender when I went out to use the privy."

"Get it. Possum, you get Tyler and Finnegan. We'll pay Slash a visit and see what Mr. Briles is up to."

This time Anders didn't announce that he was coming and didn't stop outside the door to call for Slash. He and Possum just walked right into the house, followed closely by Tyler and Finnegan, who were both cut from the same pattern: they were thin and leathery, and their eyes were as blank as a wall.

"Hey," Ella said, rising to meet them.

Lou stood up, too, holding the book she'd been reading. Anders didn't seem to notice either of them. He stormed past them. Tyler and Finnegan went with him. Possum stayed behind, holding his pistol aimed at a point about halfway between the two women.

"You'll play hell getting any from me again," Lou told Possum.

"You'll take on anybody's got five dollars," Possum said. "Now shut your mouth."

Anders pounded on the door of Slash's room. "Let me in, Slash, or I'll kick the damn door down."

"Is that you Whit? What do you want?"

"Never mind what I want. Open this door."

Slash opened the door, but only a crack. Anders shoved the door into her, knocking her back and out of the way, and entered the room, a pistol in his hand. Finnegan and Tyler stood on either side of the doorway, their guns drawn.

Fargo sat in a chair, looking puzzled.

"What in the hell's going on?" he said in his old man's voice. "Can't a man have himself a little fun without somebody breaking in and waving a pistol around under his nose?"

"Goddamn," Anders said. "What are you doing here?"

Fargo ducked his head and looked embarrassed. "I came for a poke. Hell, you oughta know. You're the one who sent me."

Anders snorted and turned to Slash. "Where is he?"

"Where is who?"

"You know goddamned well who. Briles. Where is he?"

"I haven't seen him in days. What are you talking about, Whit?"

"You never let anybody poke you. What's this old geezer doing in here?"

105

More insults, Fargo thought. Looked like being old was worse than he'd thought.

"That's none of your concern. Maybe he needed something special. You don't tell me how to run my business."

"Goddamn!" Anders said, frustration making his voice raw.

There was a modesty screen on one side of the room. A dress was draped over it.

"Goddamn!" Anders said again, and he fired two shots into the screen, which fell over forward, revealing that nothing was behind it except the wall and a little chair.

The noise filled the room and made Fargo's ears ring. The tang of powder smoke filled the air.

"Good shooting," Fargo said to Anders. "I think you killed it."

Anders whirled on him. "You say one more word and I'll shoot your nuts off, you crazy old bastard."

Fargo kept his mouth shut, trying not to smile.

"Maybe you should look under the bed, Whit," Slash said. "Maybe Briles is hiding under there."

"You go to hell. He was here. Snake saw him. What was he doing?"

"You'll have to ask Snake. He's the one who's seeing things."

"Get him," Anders said, and Tyler left the doorway and went to the back.

"Anybody come this way?" Tyler said when he opened the back door.

Snake was standing outside with his shotgun. He shook his head and said nobody had come out the back door.

"He's not downstairs," Tyler said.

"Well, I sure to God saw him go in. You tell Anders that."

Snake figured he wouldn't mention the length of time he'd been in the privy. It had taken him a while to get his business done, so it was possible that Briles had already left. If that were the case, Anders would be even madder than he was now. Snake didn't want to face Anders when he was mad.

Tyler went back and told Anders what Snake had said.

"Son of a bitch!" Anders said. "You and Finnegan go upstairs. You look in every room."

"You don't have to do that," Slash said. "Nobody's here but the girls."

"Shut the hell up," Anders said.

Finnegan and Tyler left. They came back in a few minutes with the word that Slash had been telling the truth.

"I told you Snake was seeing things," Slash said. "I'm not sure you can trust him anymore, Whit."

"He can see well enough for me to trust his eyes. I don't know what's happened, but I'll find out from Briles when I catch up with him. If he was here and you've been lying to me, you'll pay the price."

With that Anders turned and left the room. He went out the back way, Tyler and Finnegan walking fast to keep up, their boot heels clomping on the floor. Possum passed by the open door and glanced into the room. He didn't have anything to say, however, and he followed the others out of the building.

"That Anders is a friendly fella," Fargo said when the back door had slammed shut. "I don't guess you want to tell me what he was talking about."

"No," Slash said. "I don't."

She crossed the room and set up the modesty screen. Then she reached down and pulled Ella's wooden club from under the bed where she'd tossed it when Anders had started pounding on the door.

"Good thing Anders didn't look under there," Fargo said.

"I didn't think he would. If he had, I'd have thought of a reason for the club to be there." She pointed it at Fargo. "I think it would be a good idea if you left now."

Fargo ignored her last comment. He said, "Since you won't tell me what's going on, I'll tell you. I think the woman Anders is looking for was here. Not in this room, but in this house. I think she was upstairs, and that you handed her off to this Briles fella just a few minutes ago. Is that pretty much how it went?"

Slash considered him. "Even if it did, it's none of your business."

"Sure it is. I told you I came to town to get her, and I mean to do it. Looks like now I'll have to get her from Briles instead of Anders, though."

"You're a fool," Slash said, "whoever you are. So am I. I thought Briles could use the girl to hurt Whit some way. So did Briles. But we were both wrong. Anders is on his way to see Briles right now. He'll tear the saloon apart and find the girl." Her free hand went to her face, and her fingers lightly touched the scar. "Then he'll do to her what he did to me. Or worse."

Fargo stood up. "I guess I'll have to stop him."

"You just don't understand what kind of a man he is, even now, do you?"

"Maybe not, but I know he has to be stopped."

"You can't do it. One man doesn't have a chance. He'll have Snake kill you, or Possum. If you're lucky he'll kill you fast. If you're not, you'll wind up like that sheriff who came here yesterday."

Fargo thought about Stuver, hanging outside of town on the wall. He didn't want to die like that, but then he didn't think he would. He took his pack and said, "We'll see about that."

19

Katrina hadn't wanted to go with Briles, but Slash said it was for the best. Briles would protect her, Slash said. He'd be sure that Anders didn't get his hands on her.

Maybe that was true, Katrina thought, or maybe it wasn't. She'd gone with him, but she didn't trust Briles the least little bit, and now she figured that she should never have trusted Slash, either.

Katrina had gotten away from Anders by herself, and Slash had hidden her for a while, but now Briles had her. She couldn't see that she was any better off except that she had better quarters.

The big man Briles called Grunt had taken her upstairs at Briles' saloon and installed her in a very nice room that Katrina knew must have belonged to some whore that Briles had moved out.

A nice room could still be a prison, though, as she found out when she tried the door, which Grunt had locked when he left her there. Katrina was getting really tired of locked doors.

The window wasn't locked, however, but there was no help there. It opened out onto a little balcony over the street. There was no stairway down from the balcony, and Katrina couldn't possibly get outside without being seen. At least not in the daylight. Things might be different after dark, maybe sometime after midnight. It was something to consider, so she sat down on the bed and thought about it.

For his part, Briles was elated to have Katrina in the saloon. He could hardly believe his luck in getting his hands on her, even though he wasn't as yet quite sure how he'd use her. He didn't really think that Anders cared a damned thing about the girl, any more than Briles did, but he cared about not having her.

What Anders cared about was control, and he couldn't stand being thwarted. In the current situation, Anders was certainly thwarted. Losing the woman would be like losing any other possession, and he couldn't stand that. Briles thought that he might well be frustrated enough to make a mistake.

One mistake was all Briles needed, he told himself. Just one. He didn't think that Anders would trade him a saloon for the girl, though that might be a possibility.

Would it be better, he wondered, if Anders knew how Briles had come by the girl? That way, some of Anders' anger, maybe most of it, would be deflected from Briles to Slash, and that would be a good thing.

Grunt stuck his head into the office and put an end to Briles' pleasant speculations.

"Anders is on his way here," Grunt said. "He's got Finnegan and Tyler with him. Snake, too."

"Shit," Briles said.

How could Anders have found out so quickly that the woman was here? Did Slash tell him? That treacherous bitch!

The fact that he'd just been considering turning on Slash never entered Briles' mind. If it had, he wouldn't have considered it treacherous. He'd have just called it good business.

"How soon?" he said.

"They're coming down the street from Slash's place. Not long."

"Get some men together. Get ready."

"There's not enough time to get anybody rounded up."

"Do what you can, then."

Briles stood up and opened a drawer in his desk. A .44 lay inside, and he took it in his hand. He wasn't much of a hand with a pistol, but maybe he wouldn't have to use it. His mind churned as he tried to think of a way he could talk himself out of what was about to happen.

He couldn't hide the girl. There wasn't time. He could

run, but where would he go? Anders would catch him before he got out of town, and even if he got to Fort Benton, there was someone waiting to kill him. He stuck the pistol in his belt and left the room.

Briles wasn't necessarily a brave man, but if there was no place to run, he'd confront the danger and see what happened. *You never know,* he thought. *Maybe I'll get lucky and kill Anders.*

After all, that was what he'd really wanted all along. With Anders gone, Briles could take over Sundown and run it himself, the way it should be run.

That was it. Maybe he'd get lucky.

Anders and his men slammed through the bat-wing doors, pistols drawn. Snake had his shotgun at the ready.

The men in the saloon scattered. Poker chips fell to the floor, and the women screamed. The Professor kept right on playing the piano.

"Put a stop to that goddamn noise, Snake," Anders said.

Snake walked over near the piano and blasted it with the shotgun. Some men dived under tables. Others ran through the bat-wings and into the street.

The wood front of the upright piano shattered, and wires broke with a *sproing.* Smoke from the gun rose to the ceiling. The Professor fell back off his chair and lay on the floor, curled into a ball.

When the echoes of the shotgun blast died away, it was very quiet in the saloon.

Grunt and Briles walked out of the back hallway. They both held their pistols in plain sight.

"Where's the girl?" Anders said when he saw the two men.

"I don't have her," Briles told him.

"I'm getting tired of all the goddamn lying," Anders said. "I'll ask you one more time before I kill you. Where's the woman?"

It came to Briles like a flash of light. He wasn't going to get lucky. He was going to get killed. All his big plans would come to an end with a bullet from Anders' pistol.

Or he could put an end to his plans another way and stay alive. Maybe. It was worth a chance.

"She's upstairs," he said. Once he got started, the words tumbled out. "Slash had her. She asked me if I'd take her, hide her here. I said sure. Why not? I was going to give her back to you later on."

"I should just kill you where you stand, you lying bastard," Anders said.

Sweat ran into Briles' eyes. He hadn't realized how hot it was.

"You wouldn't do that. I was just trying to help you."

"I told you I was tired of the goddamn lies. Where is she?"

"I told you. Upstairs. First door on the left."

"Snake, go get her."

Snake went up the stairs, taking them two at a time with his thin legs. When he reached the door, he raised his right leg and kicked it open.

The door slammed back against the wall with a thud and bounced back. Snake plunged into the room, shotgun ready to tear apart anybody who might be hiding there to fight him.

No one was there. The window was open, and the lacy curtains fluttered in a light breeze.

Katrina had seen Anders coming down the street. She knew that couldn't be good.

The sound of the shotgun's roar shook the floor under her feet. She knew what Anders was after, and she decided at that instant that she'd better not stay in the room any longer. She pushed up the window and stepped out onto the little balcony. She was going to have to drop down to the street, just as she'd done from the window at Anders' saloon.

Several people ran out of the front of the saloon. They were so eager to get away that they didn't stop to look back and see her.

Someone saw her, however. An old man walking down the middle of the street was looking right at her.

She couldn't do anything about that. No old man was likely to stop her, and she had to get away while everyone in the saloon was occupied.

She stepped over the balcony and clung to the railing.

She was wearing a dress this time, one Slash had given her, so she was a little better protected for the fall.

She let go of the railing and fell to the street. She landed unsteadily on her feet, staggered to the side, and started to run. She didn't get far. Her ankle was hurt, and she fell. The old man stood over her, looking down at her.

"You get away from her, you old bastard," Snake yelled from the balcony.

As Katrina watched, the old man reached into a pack he was carrying and brought out a pistol. Snake saw it, too, and he pulled the trigger of the shotgun just before the man shot him.

Katrina thought she'd die instantly, but to her surprise she was hardly touched by any of the shot, and the ones that hit her merely stung, not much worse than a bee.

"Sawed-off," the old man said. "No good for anything but close work. Can you walk?"

"I'm not sure," Katrina said, wondering why the man didn't sound nearly as old as he looked.

She stood up and sagged against him. She thought her ankle was sprained, maybe broken.

"I don't think I can make it," she said.

"That's all right," he said.

He stuck his pistol in his pack and picked her up as if she were nothing more than a child. He started back up the street at a trot, just as Anders came screaming out the saloon door.

20

Briles could hardly believe he was still alive. He'd been certain that Anders was going to kill him, but the shooting had started outside, and Anders had run out, leaving Briles and Grunt standing there.

As soon as he realized that he was going to survive, Briles fired off a shot at Anders' back.

He missed, and Finnegan whirled around. Grunt shot him in the middle of the chest. Finnegan fell outside the saloon on the boardwalk.

Tyler saw him and turned back into the saloon. Grunt would have shot him, too, but Snake was coming down the stairs. Blood leaked from his shoulder, but he held the shotgun as if he were ready to use it.

Briles didn't like the odds, especially now that the shooting had begun. He turned and ran for the back door. Grunt was right behind him.

Tyler fired twice. Both bullets hit Grunt in the back, and the big man fell forward, nearly tripping up Briles as he opened the door.

Briles heard the shots. He heard Grunt's pained outcry, too, but he didn't stop to see if there was anything he could do to help him. He was too worried about his own skin to think about Grunt. He ducked out the back door and slammed it behind him just as a couple of bullets thudded into it.

For a day that had started with such promise, Briles thought, things had turned to shit awfully fast. One minute he was planning to be the big dog in Sundown, and the next he was running for his life. It seemed like things always turned around on him like that. Montana was no different from California in that regard. It wasn't fair. And where the hell was he going to hide out this time?

Fargo wasn't sure he was going to be able to get back to Slash's place. Anders and a couple of his gunmen were running after him, firing shots that cleared the street and sent the men along the boardwalk diving into doorways and alleys.

Fargo couldn't run fast while he was carrying the woman and his pack, but he wasn't about to put her down and let Anders have her. He was glad the men who were shooting at him were running, too, because it was next to impossible to hit anything while moving around like that. Still, he wished he could shoot back.

Almost as soon as he made the wish, a man up ahead stepped off the boardwalk and started shooting at Anders and his men. Fargo recognized him at once. It was Buck. He wasn't any more accurate than they were, but he was good enough to send Anders scooting for cover behind a water trough. Possum hit the dirt, and the third man, who was trailing the others, darted into an alley.

"Where you goin' so fast, Fargo?" Buck asked when Fargo reached him.

"A whorehouse."

"That's a damn good idea. You go on ahead, and I'll catch up to you."

Buck fired off a couple of shots, geysering water from the trough into the air but missing Anders completely. Then he turned and jogged after Fargo.

Fargo reached Slash's house and went inside. He put Katrina on the divan as Buck came through the door.

"What're you doing here?" Fargo asked him.

"Came to see how you was treatin' Agnes. Looks like I was just in time, too, seein' as how you've got yourself into some shootin' trouble. Looks like you could use another old man to help you out."

"I'm glad you showed up," Fargo said. "I don't reckon Anders stands a chance now."

"What's going on here?" Slash asked, entering the parlor behind them.

"I think a little war just started," Fargo said. "I'm not sure who's winning."

Slash glanced at Katrina. "You brought the girl back."

"Well, I didn't know anyplace else to go."

"This isn't the Alamo, Fargo." Slash folded her arms across her breasts. "I'm not going to let you fort up in here like a bunch of damn Texians."

The back door slammed, and Slash whirled around. "Great God almighty," she said when she saw Briles standing there. "What next?"

Briles told her what was next. "Snake's coming right behind me. Hide me."

Slash laughed at him. "He can have you for all I care, Briles, you cowardly son of a bitch."

"I thought I shot Snake," Fargo said.

"In the shoulder," Briles said. "He's still got that shotgun."

Fargo wondered if Snake could fire the gun with a wounded shoulder. If he could, and if he got close enough, he could do some serious damage.

"They killed Grunt," Briles said.

Slash said she didn't give a damn, and Fargo didn't even know who Grunt was.

"You see about Katrina," Fargo told Slash as he slipped his pistol out of the pack. "Buck, you and Briles watch out the front. I'm going to see about Snake."

He didn't wait to see if they did as he told them. He went down the hallway to the back door. He opened it slightly and peeked out the crack. He saw a couple of privies and a rain barrel. There was no sign of Snake.

That didn't mean he wasn't there. Fargo opened the door a little wider, and Snake popped up from behind the rain barrel. He held the shotgun tight against his good shoulder with both hands.

Fargo slammed the door as Snake fired. The buckshot rattled off the walls of the house, and Fargo flung the door open. Snake had dropped back down behind the barrel.

Fargo shot into the barrel near the bottom. There was water in it, and it drained out the hole.

"The barrel won't do you much good when the water's gone, Snake," Fargo said.

Snake jumped up, the shotgun pointed at Fargo's mid-section. This time Fargo didn't give Snake a chance to pull the trigger. He shot him in the bridge of the nose.

Snake's head exploded in a haze of blood and brain matter. His body fell behind the barrel, and Fargo went over to get the shotgun. He took it from Snake's limp hands and laid it beside the dead man. Then he searched through Snake's pockets and found six more cartridges. He put them into his own pockets, picked up the shotgun, and left Snake lying there, the blood and fluids from his head soaking into the dirt of the alley.

Anders lay behind the water trough and tried to assess the situation. He knew that Possum wasn't far away, but he didn't know about Finnegan and Tyler. And Snake. He'd been upstairs, and Anders had heard the shotgun fire at Katrina and the old man in the street. He didn't know what had happened after that, though.

Possum came crawling up to the trough and lay beside Anders.

"Tyler's back there behind us," Possum said when Anders asked him. "I don't know about Snake and Finnegan."

"That bastard Briles lied to me," Anders said. "Slash lied to me. Goddamn it, everybody lies to me."

Possum knew better than to respond to that.

"Katrina's in there with Slash," Anders continued. "There's a couple of men with her. They have guns, but they're in a house full of whores who won't be any help to them."

He and Possum stared at the door to Slash's place. A couple of men stood outside Anders' saloon as if they wondered what was going on.

Tyler came slinking along the walls of the building behind Anders and Possum.

"It's me," he said, and joined them on the ground.

"What about Snake?" Anders said.

"Briles went out the back. Snake went after him."

Anders figured Snake was more than a match for Briles.

"Snake's been shot," Tyler said, as if to dash any hopes Anders had.

"Shit," Anders said. "How bad?"

"Just a scratch. He'll be all right. You don't have to worry about Snake."

Anders hoped that was right. "What about Finnegan?"

"Grunt killed him. I killed Grunt. He was so damn big that he filled up the whole hallway. I couldn't get a shot at Briles."

They heard the shooting behind Slash's place: the shotgun, and then the pistol.

"I don't like the way that went," Possum said. "I never thought of Briles as much of a gunhand."

"It's not Briles that worries me," Anders said. "It's that other fella, the one who carried off Katrina. By God, he looked like that old man that was in the saloon this morning. I just talked to him at Slash's."

"That old fart couldn't carry my boots, much less a woman," Possum said.

"I wouldn't be so sure of that. It was him, by God."

There was another pistol shot, but no shotgun blast. Possum looked at Anders, who said nothing.

"Why are we lying here in the street?" Tyler said. "I need a drink."

Possum poked his head up over the top of the water trough. Nobody shot at him. He said, "I could use one, too, and not from this damn trough."

"All right," Anders said. "We'll go in the saloon. You first, Possum."

Possum didn't appear pleased with the honor, but he jumped out and ran across the street into the saloon, pushing past two men who were watching.

Seeing that Possum hadn't been shot at, Anders followed him. He stopped to speak to the men at the door.

"Fallon, you and Hart gather up four or five others and watch that whorehouse. Don't let anybody in or out. Check the alley in back and see what you find."

Fallon nodded.

"And send a couple of men out to the walls. Don't let anybody out of town unless I tell you to. Just send them on back. You got that?"

"I got it," Fallon said.

"Good. Get started."

Fallon and Hart went into the saloon to look for help. Anders went in after them, with Tyler following.

Anders waited until Fallon and Hart had gathered some men. When they had left the saloon through the back door, Anders got a bottle of the good whiskey from behind the bar and took it to a table where Tyler was already seated. Possum got three glasses and joined them.

Everyone left in the saloon ignored them, concentrating on their drinks or their poker hands. They weren't in Anders' employ, and they didn't want to get mixed up in whatever was going on.

Anders poured three drinks. He held his own glass up and studied the amber liquor as if there might be some answers located within it. If there were, he didn't find any. He drank it down.

"What do you think happened to Snake?" Possum asked when he'd downed his own whiskey.

"He'd be here by now if he'd got Briles," Tyler said. "I expect somebody got him instead."

"Shit." Possum set his glass on the table. "Me and Snake been friends a long time. You think that old man got him? The one that was in here?"

"Somebody else was shooting at us," Anders said. "Looked like another old man. The town's been invaded by goddamn geezers."

"Tough old bastards, too," Tyler said.

"If they killed Snake, they was more than tough," Possum said. "What're we gonna do about 'em?"

"We're gonna get the woman back," Anders said. "As to what happens to the geezers, I don't give a damn. I'd like to see them dead."

"Can we hang 'em? We could do it out on the wall by the sheriff."

"Good idea, but if we have to kill them, we might as well go ahead and do it, not wait around for any hanging. I don't want to take any chances with them, not if they killed Snake. If they could get him . . ."

Anders didn't finish the sentence. He didn't have to. Possum and Tyler knew what he meant.

He poured another drink for himself and handed the bottle to Possum.

21

"They'll come after us," Briles said. "This is all your fault, Slash."

Slash gave him a contemptuous look. "You're a sorry excuse for a man, Briles. I thought better of you."

Briles looked surprised. "I don't know what you're talking about."

Slash didn't respond except to sigh and shake her head.

"Forget it," Fargo said. "We don't have time for arguing. How many women are in this place?"

"Besides me and the one on the couch?" Slash asked. "Five. There's Big Tits Ella and St. Louis Lou. You've met them. Then there's Star of Texas, Montana Molly, and Pretty Penny. You've met her, too. They're all upstairs."

"Any customers up there?" Fargo said.

"Hell, no. They all left to see what the shooting was about. Two of them didn't even bother to pay."

"I figure you'll collect later."

"You can count on it. If there is a later."

"There's always a later. Can any of those girls of yours use a shotgun?"

"I can," Katrina said. "Give it here."

Fargo handed the gun to her and dug the cartridges out of his pockets. He handed them to her. She cracked the gun to check that it was loaded. Assured that it was, she snapped it shut with a click.

"Anything happening next door, Buck?" Fargo said.

"I can't see much from here, but far's I can tell, it's pretty quiet."

"They're watching us," Briles said. He wiped sweat from his forehead. "You can count on it. Anders isn't going to let us get away with this."

"What do you mean, 'us'?" Slash asked. "You're on your own, Briles. This is your fault."

"The hell it is." He jerked a thumb in Katrina's direction. "You're the one who foisted the woman off on me."

"Foisted her off?" Slash laughed. "You wanted her, and you know it. You told me yourself you were going to use her against Anders and were glad to do it."

"Stop it," Fargo said. "If you two want to fight, save it for Anders and his gunnies. Briles, do you know how to use that pistol of yours?"

"You're damn right."

"Just be sure you don't shoot me or one of my girls by accident," Slash said.

"Get them down here," Fargo told her. "The girls."

Slash went to the stairs and called. In a few seconds, the women trooped down. Fargo knew Lou, Ella, and Penny, who looked like a schoolgirl. The other two looked a little older and hard-used. They stood at the foot of the stairs, looking a little confused but not afraid. Slash explained the situation to them.

"Hey, Molly," Buck said when Slash was finished.

"You know her?" Fargo asked.

Montana Molly turned her eyes away.

"No need for that," Buck told her. "I don't blame you for not comin' back to town, not after what Anders did to Willie."

Fargo caught on then. Molly was Willie Lawrence's wife.

"Leave her alone," Slash said. "I took her in after Anders got tired of her. She's not quite used to the life here yet, but she doesn't plan to leave."

"Nothin' to be ashamed of," Buck said. "I guess you'll be glad to help us get Anders, won't you, Molly?"

Molly turned to Buck. Fargo could see that her face was flushed with anger.

"You're goddamned right I will."

"We'll all help out," Slash said. "We all have our reasons. Go to my room and get your club, Ella. It might be better than nothing."

"You don't have any guns in this place?" Buck said.

"We don't need them. We don't need a bouncer, either. We're all under Anders' protection."

"Lot of good that's gonna do you," Buck said.

Ella came back into the room and said that she'd heard somebody in the alley.

"They'll find Snake back there," Fargo said. "Be sure the door's locked."

Ella and Slash went to check, and Fargo looked around the room. He didn't trust Briles, and he had no idea about the women, except for Katrina. She looked determined, and she seemed to know what a shotgun was all about. Buck would be just fine, if he could hit what he shot at. So far Fargo hadn't seen any evidence that he could.

"I'm worried about Agnes," Buck said. "She's tied to a hitch rail out there, and she might get hurt. You shoulda taken her to the livery, Fargo."

"I didn't have a chance," Fargo said. "Let's get some furniture stacked in front of that back door, just in case they try to break in. We'd better put something at these front windows, too. Something to give us a little more protection."

"I told you this wasn't the Alamo, Fargo," Slash said. "Why don't you go somewhere else."

"Where?"

Slash didn't have an answer for that, so she and Ella went to move the washstand from Slash's room. Katrina moved to a chair, and Fargo and Briles moved the divan in front of one window. They had nothing to put in front of the other one.

"Why are you doing this?" Katrina asked Fargo. "Who are you, anyway?"

Fargo told her who he was and explained why he'd come for her.

Katrina seemed to find it hard to believe. "Because Nick helped you out in a fight, you'd risk your life to get me away from Anders?"

"I owe him," Fargo said. "I pay my debts."

"You must be crazy," Briles said. "We're all going to be killed, and you don't even have to be here."

"Yes, I do."

Briles shook his head. "Crazy, plumb crazy," he said.

Fargo wasn't crazy, but he was worried. He figured that Anders had somebody in the alley behind the whorehouse, and somebody watching the front. Nobody could get out without getting shot.

"He'll come as soon as it's dark," Briles said. "That's what he's waiting for."

It was late afternoon, and it wouldn't be long before the sun went down, but Fargo didn't think Anders would have an easy time of it if he tried to sneak up on them. The saloon was right next door, after all, and Buck was keeping a watch on it.

"What he'll do," Briles said, "is send a bunch of his men with guns. He's got us outnumbered and outgunned. We won't be able to stop 'em. They'll kill us all."

"You don't have any idea what he'll do, and you don't care what happens to us," Slash said, coming back into the parlor. "You're just scared for yourself."

"Who else do you want me to be scared for?" Briles asked. "Listen, Fargo, what you need to do is give Anders the woman. Maybe then he won't kill us. If he has her, he won't care what happens to the rest of us."

"Maybe he's right," Katrina said, her voice subdued. "I didn't mean to cause all this trouble. What can Anders do to me anyway?"

"See?" Briles said. He moved over by Katrina. "She agrees with me. Let her go, Fargo."

Katrina actually started to rise from the chair, but Slash stopped her.

"I know what you're thinking," Slash said. "All Anders can do is give you a poke or two. What harm can that do? Hell, all these girls get more than that every day."

"That's right," Katrina said. "I'll survive."

Slash touched the scar on her face. "Sure. You'll survive. But you don't know Anders like I do. You don't know how he'll treat you. When he gets through with you, not all the scars will be on your face."

Katrina shook her head. "It doesn't matter. Nick's dead. I don't want anybody else getting killed because of me."

"Too late," Slash said. "Snake's dead, too."

"Charlie Finnegan and Grunt, too," Briles said. "Anders won't stand for that. He's gonna hit us with everything he's got unless we give him the woman. Let her go if that's what she wants to do."

"I have a better idea," Fargo said.

"What's that?" Briles said.

"We'll give him you."

Briles pulled his pistol and pointed it at the back of Katrina's head.

"I'm not going anywhere. She is." He jabbed Katrina in the head with the pistol barrel. "Hand me that shotgun."

Katrina didn't have much choice, so she did as she was told. With the shotgun in hand, Briles looked more confident. He stuck his pistol in his waistband and said, "We're going to the door now. Get up."

"She can't walk," Fargo said. "She hurt her ankle."

"She can damn well hop, then," Briles said. "Get up."

Ella was in the hallway, and she stepped out with her club.

"You get back," Briles said. "If I pull this trigger, I'll cut her in half, and I still have a shot left to use on the rest of you."

Ella had raised her club, but she let her arm drop. The club dangled from her hand.

"I'll go," Katrina said.

Fargo cursed himself for not keeping a closer watch on Briles. He should never have let him get so close to Katrina.

"A man that'll hide behind a woman is low as they come," Buck said.

Briles said he didn't care what Buck thought of him. "I'll be alive," he said. "And you'll be dead."

Katrina hadn't moved out of the chair, and Briles gave her a nudge with the shotgun barrel.

"Get up," he said again, and Katrina stood.

22

Katrina's ankle wouldn't support her weight. She took one step and fell.

Ella's hand moved faster than Fargo's as he reached for his pistol. The club hit Briles' wrist with a solid crack.

Briles yelled and the shotgun dropped to the floor by Katrina, and Briles disappeared under a pile of scratching, clawing women as Lou, Molly, Star, and Penny all landed on him and carried him to the floor.

Buck watched the squirming pile while Fargo helped Katrina to her feet.

"That might be fun," Buck said to Slash. "How much do you charge for that?"

"You couldn't stand that much fun," Slash said.

She waded into the pile and started to pull the women off Briles. When she'd moved them away, Briles sat up. His face bled from numerous scratches. Ella stood over him. She said, "I'd sure like to hit your head with this club and see which of them's harder."

"No need for that," Slash said, plucking the pistol from Briles' waistband. "Tie him up, girls."

They tied him with strips of cloth torn from their clothes and left him on the floor. Fargo helped Katrina back to the chair.

"Now what're we gonna do with him?" Buck asked.

"What we started to do in the first place," Fargo said. "Offer him to Anders."

"Anders won't be satisfied," Slash said.

"Worth a try," Fargo said.

"Who'll talk to Anders about it?"

"You will," Fargo said.

125

* * *

Anders had gotten control of himself somewhat by the time the sunset caused the sky to blaze in the west. Most of the whiskey in the bottle had disappeared, and that might have contributed to his seeming calm.

"They can't get out of town," he said.

Possum sat at the table with him. Tyler had gone to check on Fallon and Hart.

"That's right," Possum said. "They couldn't get out over those rocks on ever' side of us."

"There's just the one road, and that's guarded. We have them boxed up in the whorehouse, so they can't even get out of that to get on the road. Sooner or later, they'll give up the woman."

"They killed Snake," Possum said, having gotten the word from Fallon earlier. "And Finnegan. We can't let 'em get away with that."

Anders was about to reply to that when Slash came into the saloon. Hart stood behind her, holding a pistol pointed at the middle of her back.

"She came out waving a white flag," Hart said. "She says she's got an offer for you."

"I'll just bet she has," Anders said, grinning. "What about it, Slash? You offering yourself in exchange for me letting everybody go?"

"No. It's not even my idea to be here. I'm not offering you anything. Fargo is."

"Fargo? Who's Fargo?"

"The old man that you met this morning. He said you'd remember."

"I remember him, all right. He said his name was Luke."

"He lied. He's not an old man, either. He had you fooled. He came here for the girl, and now he's got her."

Anders looked at Possum. "See what I mean? Everybody lies to me, even old geezers." He turned back to Slash. "Does he want to trade the girl for safe passage out of town?"

"No. He wants to trade you Briles."

"Why the hell would I want Briles?"

"He killed Snake," Slash said, repeating the story Fargo had given her.

"The son of a bitch," Possum said. "Take him, Anders. We'll hang the bastard on the wall in the morning."

Anders ignored him and said to Slash, "You're the one who gave Katrina to Briles, and you're right here. Why don't I just keep you?"

"Because that way you'll never get the girl."

Anders didn't like that. He started to get angry all over again.

"Get out of here, goddamn it. You tell that Fargo or Luke or whatever the hell he calls himself that I'm going to kill him. I'll kill Briles, too, and I'll kill you if I have to."

"I told Fargo that's what you'd say."

"He was a fool not to listen to you, then."

"Briles wants to take over the town from you. He was going to use the woman. You could punish him for that."

"He has about as much chance of taking this town away from me as a whore does of getting her cherry back. I can kill him anytime I want to, and I'll get him when I get the woman back. You can tell your friend Fargo that."

Slash knew she'd get nothing else from Anders. She left the saloon and went back to her own parlor, where she told Fargo what Anders had said.

"See?" Briles said. He sat propped against the wall, his hands tied behind him and his ankles bound together. The scratches on his face were no longer bleeding. "I told you it wouldn't work. Anders is going to kill us all if you don't give him the woman."

"Her name's Katrina," Fargo said.

He had never intended to give up Briles. He'd just wanted to see how Anders would respond to the offer. He should have known that Briles was right about Anders, but he had to find out for sure.

"I don't care what her name is," Briles said. "Give her up, Fargo. It's the only way we'll get out of this."

"No, it's not," Fargo said.

"I'd sure admire to hear how you're going to work it, then," Buck said. " 'Cause all I know about is a street out front and an alley out back. Ain't neither one of 'em offerin' us a way out of here."

"There's a way," Fargo said, though he didn't know exactly what it was.

"You gonna tell us?"

"I don't know yet," Fargo said. He had some ideas, but he didn't want to tell everybody else, not yet. "We'll keep a watch and see what Anders tries to do. He can't come after us any easier than we can go after him."

"We could give that a try," Buck said. "We'll just go over there and take him on."

Briles snorted. He was on the verge of saying something when there was a noise from upstairs. Fargo had stationed the other women up there at the windows in case Anders' men tried to get in that way. The balcony that ran in front of the second-floor windows of the saloon was only a few feet from the one on the whorehouse. A man could jump from one to the other easily enough.

"Stay here," Fargo told Buck and ran upstairs.

He went into the front room on the left of the hallway and found Big Tits Ella swinging her club at a man who had drawn his pistol on her. She didn't appear to be afraid of him, and one man already lay on the floor near the window, where he'd fallen. Ella had probably hit him as he came in, but the other man had been following so closely that she missed.

The other women were nowhere to be seen. Fargo figured they'd run at the first sign of trouble.

The man with the pistol saw Fargo and snapped off a quick shot. The bullet tugged at Fargo's loose clothing and buried itself in the wall.

The man ducked out the window. He landed on the balcony and was about to climb up on the rail and jump back to the saloon when Fargo caught up with him.

The man swung around and hit Fargo on the side of the head with the pistol.

Fargo fell against the side rail and the man hit him again, hoping to cause him to fall over.

He almost succeeded. Fargo leaned out, then snapped back, ducking the pistol this time and aiming a punch at the man's chest.

He hit it solidly, and the man's breath came out in a

whoosh as he slammed against the whorehouse wall. Fargo sprang forward and took the pistol. Then he grabbed the man's shirtfront and spun around, throwing him over the rail.

The man hit the street with a dull thud, but Fargo didn't look down to see if he was alive. He went back through the window.

The man Ella had clubbed still lay motionless on the floor, and Ella stood by with her club. Fargo took the man's pistol. Now he had three. At this rate, he was going to be better armed than Anders' whole gang.

"Did you kill him, Ella?" he said.

"Don't give a damn if I did," she answered.

Fargo felt for a pulse and found it, faint but present.

"Wrap him up in a blanket and tie him," he said. "Do you want a pistol?"

Ella hefted her club. "This is all I need."

Fargo left her there and went into the room across the hall where Lou and the other women were.

"Which two of you can handle a pistol?" he said.

"I can," Lou told him. "Give Molly one, too."

"Damn right," Molly said. "Anybody else comes sneaking around here's gonna get shot in the brisket. I just hope it's Anders."

Fargo figured they could at least scare somebody, if not kill them. He went back downstairs.

"Untie me and give me my gun back," Briles said when he saw Fargo. "I can help you out. I don't want to die on the floor, trussed up like this."

"We can't trust you," Fargo said. "Slash can keep the gun."

"Goddamn it, you'll get us all killed."

"Maybe not. We're wearing them down. Ella has one upstairs, and there's one in the street."

"Saw him when he passed by the window," Buck said. "He's hurt pretty bad, but he was able to get up and limp off. Don't think he'll be back, though." He looked around at Slash. "You got anything to eat in this place?"

"We have a kitchen. Penny can cook a little."

Buck grinned. "Sure could do with some bacon and beans."

"I'll tell Penny. She might even make biscuits."

"Shit," Briles said. "We're all gonna die, and you're worried about eating."

"Don't want to die on an empty stomach," Buck said.

Fargo couldn't say that he blamed him.

"You want something, Fargo?" Slash asked.

"Sure. First I want to have a talk with the man Ella's tied up. That is, if he can talk yet. She hit him pretty hard."

"Send Penny down when you go up there."

Fargo said he would.

The man who lay on the floor said his name was Tyler. He also mentioned that his head hurt like hell and that he wanted a drink. Fargo said he could have some water and sent Ella for it. She'd wrapped Tyler in a blanket, and then rolled up a sheet and tied it around him. He wouldn't be going anywhere.

"What's Anders' plan?" Fargo asked him.

"Damned if I know," Tyler said. "Ain't there some way you can set me up? I can't even wiggle my damn fingers."

"Maybe I could," Fargo told him. "If I knew what Anders had in mind for us."

Tyler didn't answer. Fargo sat on the bed and waited until Ella came back with a cup of water. Fargo took the cup from her and squatted down beside Tyler.

"Be mighty hard to drink, lying down like that," Fargo said. "Probably spill every drop."

Tyler's tongue flickered out between his dry lips, then disappeared.

"I gotta have a drink," he said. "Help me sit up."

"Anders' plans," Fargo said. "I need to know what he's going to do."

"He'd kill me."

"How much chance do you think you have if you don't tell me? You're wrapped up like a pig in a blanket, and Ella's standing there with her club. When Anders comes after us, she's going to bash your brains out on the floor unless we have some kind of a chance ourselves."

"Shit, you don't give a man much of a choice."

"No," Fargo said. "I don't."

23

After midnight, Fargo and Slash sat in her room. Buck was watching the front, and Lou was at the back door, but there'd been no attack by Anders. It had been a quiet night so far, just as Tyler had said it would be.

"Do you think he'll try something before morning?" she said.

"Not unless Tyler was lying to me," Fargo said, "and I don't think he was, not with Ella and her club there to keep him on the straight and narrow."

There had been activity in some of the buildings across the street, but that fit in with Tyler's story.

"Anders'll wait until morning," Fargo said. "He's been getting men into position tonight. Tomorrow they'll open up on us."

"What are we going to do about it?"

Fargo thought that was a good question, and he still didn't have an answer, not one that satisfied him. He was worried about how many innocent men he might kill. That is, if there were any innocent men in Sundown at all.

He could have told Slash something just to comfort her, but he'd started to like her, at least a little, and he didn't want to lie. So he told the truth.

"I don't know. We'll have a little advantage on them since they're on the west side of the street and maybe the sun will be in their eyes. I still think Anders should be satisfied with Briles. I'd be glad to get rid of him."

Briles had been whining and complaining all evening. He told them about his big plans and how he'd run Sundown when he took over. He talked about his bad luck and begged them to cut him loose.

131

"People make their own luck," Fargo had told him, but even that didn't shut Briles up.

"I'd be glad to be shut of him, too," Slash said. "Anders doesn't want him any more than we do, though."

Fargo nodded. "I don't blame him."

Slash gave a little laugh. "Me neither. I wish something would happen. Waiting's worse than the thing you're waiting for."

Fargo grinned. "I can think of a few ways to pass the time."

Slash sobered and touched the scar on her face. "You don't mean that."

"Sure I do. What better way than to pass some time with a pretty woman?"

"I'm not pretty."

"I don't know why you'd say that. You're prettier than anybody in this house."

Slash looked at him. "Even Katrina?"

"Even her. She's a little too young and inexperienced. You look like a woman who knows her way around, and that gives you a look she can't match yet."

"You have a smooth tongue, Fargo."

"You don't know the half of it. How'd you like to find out?"

Slash turned away, hiding the scar from him. "You shouldn't tease."

"I'm not teasing," Fargo said. "Try me and see."

"Maybe you're too old for me."

"You know better than that," Fargo said, "but I'm willing to prove it if you want me to."

"I . . . don't do that anymore."

"Haven't you wanted to? Now and then, anyway?"

She turned to face him again. "God, yes. Especially now. You remember what Buck said about not wanting to die on an empty stomach?"

Fargo nodded.

"Well, I don't want to die with something else empty. I'd like to get it filled up one more time. Can you fill it up, Fargo?"

"I'd be mighty happy to try."

"Blow out the lamp, then."

Fargo didn't ask why. He figured he knew, so he blew out the lamp and got undressed.

"Can you find your way to the bed?" Slash asked.

"I think I can manage."

Fargo moved from the chair to the bed and lay down on it with her. They didn't move for a few seconds, and then Fargo turned and touched her. He went no farther than her nipples, which were rock-hard. He caressed them gently for a while before letting his fingers drift lower. They hadn't gone far before they encountered the first scar.

"Don't," Slash said.

"It's all right," Fargo told her. "It doesn't mean a thing if you don't let it."

She didn't say any more, and his fingers traced the scar. He was sure it had been left by a whip. Just another reason why Anders needed to be taken care of.

Fargo's fingers moved on down. There was another scar on her stomach, but she didn't say anything. Neither did Fargo. He let his fingers slide to the curling hair around Slash's nether lips, which parted instantly.

"Ahhh," she said. "It's been so long."

She was wet and slick, and Fargo's finger glided easily over the rigid button that was the source of her pleasure. She moaned and put her hand over his.

"Faster," she said. "Faster."

Fargo's finger slipped up and down rapidly. Slash could hardly contain herself as she thrashed on the bed. She pushed his hand lower, and his finger slipped into her. She spasmed instantly.

"Ahh," she sighed.

Fargo removed his hand, but she forced it back with her own.

"That was too fast," she said. "I knew it had been a long time, but I didn't realize just how much I missed it. Start over."

Fargo didn't need any further urging, but this time, while his fingers were working down below, he applied his lips and tongue to her nipples. Her excitement mounted by the second, but then she moved Fargo's hand away.

"I almost forgot about you," she said, reaching for his shaft.

She wrapped her fingers around it and said, "You certainly aren't an old man, Fargo. Not with a tool as stiff as that. Lie back."

He did, and she applied her hot mouth to him, taking him in a little at a time, working up and down, occasionally working him with her tongue alone. It might have been a while, but she hadn't forgotten a thing. He could vouch for that. In fact, if she didn't stop what she was doing, she'd know for sure how effective she was.

She did stop. She lay back on the bed and said, "I'm ready for the real thing, Fargo. Fill me up."

Fargo did his best. His stiff rod slipped into her easily, and he let it go all the way.

"That's right," Slash said. "Now work it."

Fargo worked it. Slowly, then faster, then slowly again. Slash worked with him, twisting her hips as expertly as if she'd been doing it every day for years. Soon they were both in a near frenzy, and Fargo could hold back no longer. Gushers erupted from him, one shot after another, as Slash bucked beneath him, her body shuddering in orgasm after orgasm.

When it was over they lay side by side. Slash said, "Thank you, Fargo."

"I'm the one who should be thanking you."

"No. You made me realize what a fool I've been about myself. You proved to me tonight that you're right about the scars. They haven't changed a thing about me, not really. Even if Anders kills me, I can die happy knowing that."

"Anders isn't going to kill anybody," Fargo said.

"I wish I believed that."

Fargo wished he believed it himself. He got dressed and went to check on Tyler, who was still trussed up and not going to bother anybody. He was asleep on the floor, snoring like a hog. Ella was asleep in a chair nearby, her club lying across her lap.

Downstairs, Briles was awake. He was propped against the wall, and when Fargo walked into the parlor, he and Buck were discussing how much chance Buck might have of persuading one of the whores to give him a free sample.

"I'd say not a chance in hell," Briles said. "They're in it for the money, not to comfort an old coot like you."

"Might be the last chance they ever get to comfort anybody," Buck said. "I got a feeling it worked for somebody I know."

He gave Fargo a big grin, revealing all ten of his good teeth.

"I'd keep my mouth shut as much as I could when I was talking to them," Fargo told him. "That might help."

"I don't really give a damn if he gets him any or not," Briles said. "But I know it ain't right to let a man die tied up like this. The least you could do is give me a fighting chance to get out of this mess alive."

Fargo didn't much like Briles, and he certainly didn't trust him. Briles was as slimy a character as Fargo had run across lately, and he'd do whatever was to his own advantage, not giving a damn about anybody else. However, now that all Anders' men were in position, there might be a job that Briles could do.

"What do you know about blasting powder?" Fargo asked.

The way Tyler had explained Anders' plan to Fargo, Anders didn't have nearly as many men who'd help him out as people might have thought. Most of the men in Sundown were paying good money to stay there, and they were spending the rest of their money in the saloons and whorehouses that Anders had an interest in. They thought that was all they owed him, and they didn't want to get involved in a shooting war that might get them killed.

Even at that, however, Anders had Fargo's little crew well outnumbered, and the men were all killers and owlhoots who didn't put much of a value on anybody's life but their own, and sometimes not even that. A few whores and an old man and Fargo wouldn't stand a chance against a bunch like that.

Fargo had known that before he ever left Fort Benton,

so he'd tried to think of a way to give himself a little advantage. That's when he'd thought of the blasting powder. A town like Fort Benton was likely to have a good supply of it, what with the storekeepers wanting to cater to the miners passing through, and Fargo didn't have any trouble getting his hands on some. He'd bought it and stowed it away in his pack before leaving Fort Benton.

No matter what Anders thought Fargo might do, the Trailsman was sure that the idea of blasting powder would never enter his mind. Which meant that Fargo would have a good chance to surprise him.

When and how he'd surprise Anders had been on Fargo's mind all night. He didn't want to kill a lot of people who had no part in the fighting. Not that they weren't guilty of something or other, considering the kind of place Sundown was, but it went against Fargo's grain to kill people who weren't trying to hurt him. On the other hand, he didn't much care what happened to people who were trying to kill him.

What he'd have preferred to do was blow up the building across the street from Slash's house, but there was no way to get there. According to Tyler, the back door of the whorehouse was being watched as closely as the front door. Even if someone could get outside, he'd never get across the street.

When the sun came up, Anders would attack from the front. He'd hope that everyone in the house would go out the back, and the men stationed there would cut them down.

If that didn't work, Anders figured the attack on the front would be so fierce that nobody would be left to defend the rear, and his men would break down the door and come in that way.

It all sounded likely to Fargo, and he believed Tyler was telling the truth.

So what was he going to do about it?

That was where Briles came in. And the blasting powder.

"I never worked in a mine, if that's what you mean," Briles said when Fargo asked him about the blasting powder.

136

"I have," Buck said. "Ain't anybody in this territory knows more about powder than I do. You want a powder monkey, I'm your man."

"I want you at that window," Fargo said. "With your gun."

The Trailsman trusted Briles with the powder, but not with a weapon. He might be making a mistake, but he thought he knew how to persuade Briles to do the job he wanted him to do.

"Well, Briles?" he said.

"I know enough to set off a charge. That's about all."

"That's enough. Buck, if you were going to blow up a building, how would you go about it?"

Buck rubbed the stubble on his face and said he'd try to take out the supports. "That way the place would collapse. You got small-grained powder?"

"Big-grained."

"Good. Better for the kind of job you want to do. Blows things up in the air instead of collapsin' 'em. You put the powder under the supports in the buildin', and it'll collapse sure enough, but that big-grained powder will blow out the walls if you use enough of it. The saloon'll scatter over half the town."

That sounded good to Fargo. He said, "Tell Briles what to do."

"You got fuses?"

Fargo said that he had them.

"You don't want to get trapped under there, Briles," Buck said.

"I haven't agreed to do anything yet." Sweat stood out on Briles' forehead. He stiffened against the wall. "I'm not so sure about this."

"I'll tell you what, Briles," Fargo said. "You either do it, or I'm going to cut you loose in the morning when the shooting starts."

"That's better," Briles said. He relaxed a little.

"You didn't let me finish," Fargo told him. "As soon as I cut you loose, I'm going to kick your ass out the door. Put you right out there in the middle of the street. Maybe Anders will waste a lot of his ammunition on you."

"You wouldn't do that."

"The hell I wouldn't."

The look on Fargo's face must have convinced Briles that the Trailsman would do exactly what he said.

"What do you want me to do?" he asked.

Fargo told him, and Buck gave him instructions on how to carry out the plan.

"What if it doesn't work?" Briles wanted to know.

"We'll probably all get killed," Fargo said. "Either that or Anders will hang us up out there with Sheriff Stuver."

"Be better to get blowed up than have that happen to you," Buck said.

"All right, goddamn it. I'll do it."

"I thought you might," Fargo said.

24

It was hot and close under the floor of Anders' saloon. The pervasive smell of dirt reminded Briles of funerals and open graves as he slithered along.

He'd gotten out of the whorehouse through a hole that Fargo had made in the floor, and since the house was so close to the saloon, there wasn't much chance of anyone seeing him as he crossed over the gap between them. He pulled Fargo's pack along with him.

He hoped he knew what he was doing. He wiped sweat from his eyes with the back of his hand. There wasn't a lot of working room under the floor, and he'd already bumped his head once. He didn't figure anybody had heard him, though. Nobody would be in the saloon, or that's what he'd told Fargo. He didn't know if it was the truth, but Briles didn't give a damn about anybody who might be inside.

He found a hole at each of the central supports where he could tamp in the powder, putting in what he hoped was close to the amount Buck had told him. Once the powder was in, he inserted a fuse. Then he filled up the rest of the hole with dirt, packing it as tightly as he could, leaving room for the fuse to get a little air.

When he was out of powder, he made sure all the fuses were connected and slithered back the way he'd come.

He was feeling much more optimistic than he had earlier. He'd been sure Fargo would kill him or hand him over to Anders, but now things were looking up.

Fargo would have to trust him now, maybe even give him a gun. If Fargo's plan worked, that was all well and good. Briles would be left in Sundown to pick up the pieces after Anders was dead, and the town would be Briles'. Maybe someone else would try to take over, but Briles didn't think anyone had the ability or the intelligence to do it. If somebody got in his way, he'd eliminate him.

On the other hand, if Fargo's plan didn't work, Anders would still be around, so Briles had to consider that eventuality. First of all, he'd have to convince Fargo to give him his gun back. If he could do that, and later it looked like Anders was going to win, Briles would either kill or capture Fargo, and claim that he'd been forced to go against Anders. He didn't feel there was any shame attached to such an idea. Hell, Fargo had tried to give him to Anders, so whatever he did to Fargo was fair payback.

If Anders and Briles both survived, Briles wouldn't be running Sundown, but as long as Briles could stay alive, he'd be satisfied. A man had to look out for himself.

Briles poked his head up through the floor of the whorehouse.

"Poppin' in like a mouse out of a hole," Buck said with a cackle. "I could've shot your head off there before you ever knew it."

Briles didn't see the humor in the remark. He said, "There's a little problem with the fuse."

"Tell me," Fargo said.

"It's not quite long enough. Somebody's going to have to go back down and light it."

"I'll do it," Slash said as she came into the parlor. "I can't think of anything that would make me happier than to blow up Anders' saloon."

"How about shooting him?" Katrina asked, giving the shotgun a little lift from her lap.

"Yeah," Slash said. "That would be fine, too."

Briles perked up when Slash volunteered to light the fuse. He couldn't have hoped for a better outcome, and he didn't waste any time.

"If you're down there lighting the fuse, I should be using my pistol up here," he said. "How about letting me have it back?"

Slash looked at Fargo, who said he'd think about it.

"When do you want me to light the fuse?" Slash asked.

"When the first shots are fired," Fargo told her.

He thought they could hold out while the fuses burned. When the explosions began and the saloon started to fly apart, Fargo planned to go on the attack himself, hoping that Anders and his gunhands would be so confused that they'd stop shooting for long enough to let Fargo cross the street.

Once he got across, he was going after Anders, the one man who had to be stopped. With Anders out of the way, the rest of the men would give up.

Or so Fargo hoped. He knew he had only a slim chance of getting to Anders, but it was about the only one he had.

He wanted to talk to Katrina and Buck, so he asked Slash to take Briles back to the kitchen.

"Shoot him if he gives you any trouble," Fargo added.

"That would be almost as good as shooting Anders," Slash said.

Briles glared at her, but she just smiled. When they left the room, Fargo turned to Katrina.

"I'm thinking of letting Briles have the pistol," he said. "If I do, I want you to watch him. If he tries anything, I want you to pull the trigger on him. Can you do it?"

"I can do it." Katrina's eyes were cold. "You don't have to worry about me."

Fargo believed her.

"You watch him, too, Buck," Fargo said.

"Hell, you don't have to tell me. I've been watchin' buzzards like that since you were a pup. Longer, even."

Fargo grinned and went into the kitchen. Briles was drinking coffee while Slash sat across from him, holding the pistol.

"I get the feeling you two don't trust me," Briles said. "Believe me, I want to get out of this as much as you do. I'll hold up my end."

"We'll find out," Fargo said. "Slash, before you go to light the fuse, give him the pistol."

Slash frowned. "I don't think that's a very good idea, Fargo."

"We'll have to chance it. Briles, you go to the parlor and get at the window on the right. Slash will hand you the gun."

Briles arched his eyebrows. "That's the unprotected window."

"If you'd rather meet Anders out in the street," Fargo said, "we can do it that way."

Briles grumbled a little more, but then he gave in.

"All right, I'll do it your way. Just give me the pistol."

He reached for it, but Slash moved it out of the way.

"Not until it's time," she said. "Not until you're at the window. Finish your coffee."

Briles didn't argue. He picked up the coffee mug again and took a sip.

Just before the sky started turning pink in the east, Fargo went upstairs. Molly and Penny were there in the front bedroom, staring out the window.

"It won't be long," Fargo said. "You two stay out of sight. Molly, don't waste any bullets. If anybody tries to come in through the window, shoot him. Otherwise, hold off."

"I'd sure like to shoot a few of them," she said. "Anders especially."

Fargo told her about the little surprise he'd arranged for Anders.

"What if we blow up, too?" Penny said.

"That's the chance we're taking. If Anders' men run out in the street, Molly, go ahead and take a shot at them."

Molly nodded. Fargo didn't have much confidence that she could hit anybody from up there above the street, but she might get in a lucky shot.

"I'll be out there, too," he said. "Try not to shoot me."

"You don't have to worry," she told him, but he worried just the same.

Fargo went back downstairs and found Ella and Lou at the back door. Fargo explained what was going to happen.

"Whoever's out there watching the alley will be

142

scared," he said to Ella. "You might get a chance to wade into them with that club. It's dangerous, and you don't have to try it if you don't want to."

"I'll go with her," Lou said. "I have six shots here, and I'm gonna make 'em count."

"You might both just get killed."

"Maybe. What the hell. It's better than not doing anything. Anders has had us under his thumb for too long. It's time we did something about it."

Fargo wished them luck and went back to the parlor.

"It's time for you to go," he told Slash. "Give Briles the pistol. Then light the fuse just as soon as the first shot's fired."

"Where's the end of the fuse?" Slash asked Briles.

"It's right at the edge of the saloon. You'll have to reach for it."

"Just slip on over," Fargo said. "It'll be just about daylight by then. Don't linger in the gap."

"I'll be quick," Slash said.

She slipped through the hole in the floor. Just before she ducked her head down, Buck said, "You sing out when you're coming back. I don't want to pop you."

"That's what I like about you, Buck," Fargo said. "You're always a bundle of sunshine."

25

Slash didn't think about open graves when she was under the buildings. She was reminded of when she was a little girl. She'd followed her father in the fields as he plowed up the earth, and she'd always liked the smell of fresh dirt. She hadn't been a girl for a long time, however, and she hardly remembered what her father looked like.

When she slipped under the saloon, she located the fuse and laid down the lucifers she'd held in her hand. All she had to do now was wait for the sound of gunfire.

The sky brightened, and Slash could see the shadows in the gap diminish. She wondered for just a second what it would be like to stay where she was after she lit the fuse, to just let the building come down on top of her, or be blown up with it. She pushed the thought out of her mind. She might be nothing more than a scarred whore to Anders, but Fargo had convinced her that she was somehow more than that.

When the shooting started, it surprised her. It wasn't as loud as she'd expected it to be. She lit the first match and touched it to the fuse, which started fizzing. She watched it spark and sputter for a second or two to be sure that it wouldn't go out, and when it didn't she slipped back under the whorehouse.

"I'm coming in," she said.

"Come ahead!" Buck shouted.

She stood up and climbed out of the hole. The firing sounded louder now, and a bullet crashed through the window and into the wall near her. Fargo gave her a pistol and said, "Keep down, and don't waste a shot. We don't have much ammunition. Wait for the blowup."

A couple of bullets whacked into the front walls. One buried itself in the divan, making Buck flinch.

"We might not live that long," he said.

"Are you sure you lit that fuse?" Briles said.

"It was lit when I left," Slash told him.

More shots came from across the street. Glass broke upstairs. The walls were being riddled with bullets.

"This place ain't gonna hold up much longer," Buck said. "The walls'll just fall down on us."

"Hang on," Fargo said.

"It's not going to work," Briles said. He was sweating heavily. "She didn't light the fuse, or maybe it went out, but it's not going to work."

He'd barely gotten the last word out when the first explosion came. It was followed by another and another and another.

The whorehouse shook. Boards pounded its sides and flew across the street as the entire front of the saloon exploded outward. Pieces of debris rained down and black smoke rose into the morning air.

Fargo didn't wait. Almost as soon as the blasts began, he was out of the door and running across the street. His ears rang, and he wouldn't have heard shots if they'd been fired at him. He could barely hear the sound of his own .44 as it hammered out a shot at a man who poked his head out a window.

The man's head snapped back and he disappeared inside the building. Another man stepped out the door. Fargo shot him in the chest. A third man stepped out. He fell before Fargo could pull the trigger.

Fargo looked back. Buck was coming along behind him. Briles was nowhere to be seen.

I should have known better than to think that bastard would help, Fargo thought.

A man fell from the balcony and landed in front of Fargo. He glanced back again. Molly stood on the opposite balcony with a smoking pistol in her hand. She was a better shot than Fargo would have guessed. He ran on toward the building where Anders was holed up.

*   *   *

Anders sat in a room at the back of the building with Possum. They weren't doing any of the fighting. Anders preferred to leave that to others. He didn't mind killing. He just didn't see the need to take any risks. He'd been surprised and confused by the explosions, but he caught on fast.

"The son of a bitch blew up my main saloon," he said.

Then he realized that his men were being shot. He jumped up and opened the door of the room.

"Don't go outside!" he yelled. "Fargo's out there!"

"That son of a bitch," Possum said. "I'll get him."

"Don't," Anders said, but Possum was already gone.

Ella shoved open the back door of the whorehouse while planks from the saloon were still clattering down. Lou stepped out and shot a man as he came around the outhouse, which was now canted over sideways. She shot a second as he tried to run away down the alley.

"Get their pistols," she told Ella.

Ella ran and grabbed them. She had to put down her club to hold one in each hand. Neither one had been fired.

"Take 'em to Slash," Molly said. "I'll watch the alley."

Ella ran back into the house. She gave one pistol to Slash and kept one for herself.

"What the hell's he doing here?" she said, looking at Briles. "Why aren't you out there helping Fargo?

"I was just leaving," Briles said.

Briles stood up and rushed out the front door.

"What do you think?" Ella said.

"I don't trust him. I'm going after him."

Slash went out behind Briles. Katrina stood up, holding the shotgun.

"I'm going, too," she said.

"You can't even walk," Ella said.

"I'll manage," Katrina told her and followed Slash out the door.

Anders' men had started to shoot again, and the street was dangerous. Briles knew that Fargo had been wrong.

146

They didn't stand a chance. He was going to have to kill Fargo now to let Anders know whose side he was on.

He didn't have a chance to do anything because Possum came out of the saloon, took a look at the street, and shot him. Briles looked surprised and fell in the street.

Fargo was surprised, too, because Possum had been shooting at him and missed.

"Shit," Possum said.

Seeing that his shot had gone wrong, he ducked back inside. Fargo kept right on going. He knew Buck was behind him, but he didn't know about Slash and Katrina, who was hobbling along on her bad ankle.

A bullet ripped through the sleeve of Slash's dress, but she didn't slow down. She was right behind Fargo and Buck when they burst through the door. Nobody stopped to check on Briles.

The building was another saloon. Fargo saw a man on the stairs and shot him. Buck picked off one who looked up over the top of the bar, and Slash shot one, who tumbled over the balcony rail and landed on the faro table below, splitting the face of the tiger right in two.

Fargo heard something behind him and looked around just as Katrina came in.

"Briles is out there in the street," she said. "He's hit."

Fargo didn't care. "Who's left at your place?" he asked Slash.

"Everybody else. They'll be all right."

"How many more men you reckon are in here?" Buck said.

Fargo didn't have any idea, but he knew Anders was around somewhere. So was Possum.

Fargo had to find them.

26

Anders was no longer around. He had left the back room and slipped out the door into the alley almost as soon as Possum went out to confront Fargo.

Possum had returned to find Anders gone. Possum was alone in the room, sweating and swearing to himself while he waited for Fargo to come looking for him. He sat in a chair facing the door with his pistol in his hand. It was cocked and ready.

Possum didn't even plan to wait until Fargo came into the room. As soon as he heard a sound outside, he'd shoot through the door.

He could hear them talking out there in the saloon, Fargo and some others, and he figured it wouldn't take them long to start searching. He noticed that his right leg was trembling, and he pressed his foot to the floor to stop it.

Fargo stood in the big room and looked up at the second floor. He didn't see any movement, but he knew there'd be some more men up there. If they tried to go out over the balcony, Molly would shoot at them, but they might be able to get out the back if there were any windows.

He and Buck reloaded their pistols. When he was finished with his, Fargo said to Katrina and Slash, "Buck and I will go upstairs. You two stay down here. Shoot anybody you see except us."

"What about Briles?" Slash said. "He's still out in the street."

"Leave him. If he's dead, it won't matter. If he's not, we'll worry about him later."

Slash nodded, and Fargo went up the stairs with Buck practically walking on his heels. When they got to the second floor, Fargo went to the first door, which was open. The man who'd fallen over the balcony had been in that room, and it was now empty. That left three more doors.

Fargo moved to the next one. He stood on the left of it, and Buck took the right side. Buck rattled the knob. Nothing happened, so Buck turned the knob and gave the door a good shove.

Two guns cracked off shots, and two bullets buzzed through the doorway. Fargo moved in front of the door. Trask and Zack were behind the bed.

Fargo didn't waste time greeting them. He shot Trask, who fell forward on the bed, staining the cover red, and Zack ducked down to hide. He fired from underneath the bed, trying for Fargo's ankle, but the bullet plowed along the floor, gouging up the wood.

Fargo took two long steps and jumped onto the bed, causing Trask to bounce. Zack looked up from the floor, and Fargo shot him in the eye.

Buck had stepped into the room, but he kept a watch out the door, which was a good thing. A man came out of the room next door and looked toward the gunshots. He took a couple of steps forward, and when he got close, Buck stepped out of the room and shot him in the chest. He blundered back against the wall and slid down it, trailing blood.

"We're making a hell of a mess," Buck said as Fargo came to the door.

"Too bad," Fargo said. "But we don't have to clean it up. Let's check the room he came from."

Nobody else was inside the room, so they moved to the last one. When Buck pushed the door open, a man ducked through the window and onto the balcony. Two shots came from across the street.

Fargo went to the window. The man lay flat on his face. Fargo looked across at Molly, who gave him a jaunty wave. Fargo waved back and turned to Buck.

"Where the hell's Anders?" Buck said.

Fargo didn't know. He didn't know where Possum was, either.

"Anders must be downstairs," he said. "Let's go find out."

But it was already too late.

When Anders left the saloon, he went to the side of the building and sidled along the gap between it and the next. Nobody could see him from across the street because of the angle. Ignoring all the shooting above his head, he reached the boardwalk, slipped under the overhanging balcony, and stuck close to the wall, remaining invisible to any watchers from the whorehouse.

He reached the door of the saloon and took a look inside. He saw Katrina and Slash. The shotgun worried him a little, but both women had their backs to him. He stepped in just as Fargo and Buck started to come back down.

"Just stop where you are," Anders called up to them, holding his pistol pointed in the general direction of Slash and Katrina. "Lay your pistols on the floor. If you don't, I'll kill both these women."

Slash started to turn.

"Uh-uh," Anders said. "Put the pistol on the floor. Katrina, you put the shotgun down."

"What're we gonna do, Fargo?" Buck said.

"We'll do what he said."

Fargo laid his pistol on the floor, and Buck did the same, though he didn't look too happy about it. Fargo didn't blame him. Below, the women followed suit.

"That's fine," Anders said when all the guns were on the floor. "Come down here now, Fargo, and bring your friend with you."

When Fargo and Buck got to the foot of the stairs, Anders told them to stop. Then he called out for Possum to get his ass in there.

Possum came from the back room, pistol ready, looking relieved that he hadn't been forced to confront Fargo alone. His leg had stopped trembling. When he saw what the situation was, he grinned like the animal that had given him his nickname.

"Goddamn," he said. "I thought for a while there we was in big trouble, but it looks like ever'thing has sure enough turned out all right."

"It's not all right," Anders said. "How many dead men are in here?"

Possum's grin disappeared, and he shook his head.

"I didn't count," Fargo said.

"You're a liar, but I don't care. Here's what we'll do. Slash, you'll tell those women across the street to put down any weapons they have."

"Why should I do that?"

"Because if you don't, I'll kill you where you stand."

Slash shrugged. "Go ahead."

"You always were stubborn," Anders said with a hint of admiration. "All right. I won't kill you. I'll kill Katrina instead. I don't think I want her around me anyway. I'll go back to Fort Benton and get me somebody else."

"Goddamn you, Anders," Slash said. "Don't shoot her. I'll tell them."

"I thought you would."

"What about Fargo?" Possum said. "Can I have him?"

"I don't see why not. Son of a bitch blowed up my favorite saloon."

It was very quiet outside the building. Fargo wondered where everybody was. The other men in town should be drifting along soon to see the result of the fighting. They wouldn't be any help, though, even if they did show up. They'd all be on Anders' side.

He looked at Possum. Possum grinned.

Briles stood up. It seemed to take him a long time. The front of his shirt was covered with dirt and blood, and there was a deep ache in his side. He could barely stand.

He *was* standing, however, and he still had his pistol, though it wasn't easy to keep a grip on it. He started to move in the direction of the saloon.

Slash saw him coming as she left. She stepped off the boardwalk into the street and put her finger to her lips to shush him.

He didn't know why she did that, but it didn't matter. He couldn't have made a sound if he'd tried. Walking was hard enough.

Slash kept going across the street, and Briles shuffled forward, his knees bent. He wasn't sure he could hold up the pistol much longer.

Somehow he got to the boardwalk and took the step up onto it.

"I'm gonna kill you slow," Possum told Fargo. He gestured with his pistol. "Maybe start with the feet, then the knees. I've heard being shot in the foot hurts like hell. Time I get to your heart, you'll be begging me to finish you."

Fargo didn't plan on doing any begging, but he didn't tell Possum. No need to upset him.

"Get on with it," Anders said, just as Briles' shoes scraped on the boardwalk behind him.

Anders whirled, saw Briles, and took a shot at him.

Possum was distracted for an instant, and that was all Fargo needed. He reached into his boot, whipped out the Arkansas toothpick, and jammed it into Possum's thin belly.

A look of great surprise crossed Possum's face. His eyes widened. They widened even further as Fargo jerked the knife upward, slicing through muscles and flesh.

All Possum said was, "Oh."

He dropped his pistol, and Fargo pulled back his knife. Possum's hands went to his belly to hold in his guts. Fargo pushed him away. Possum fell to his knees, looking as if he couldn't believe what he was seeing and feeling.

Anders missed Briles because Briles had already been falling when Anders pulled the trigger. Briles sagged against the door frame, and the pistol dropped from his fingers.

Anders turned back to see Fargo push Possum away. He also saw that Katrina was holding the shotgun again and that it was pointed right at him. So he shot her.

She fell backward and dropped the shotgun. By that time Fargo had snatched up Possum's pistol, and Buck had grabbed the one Slash had put on the floor.

"Looks like we got us a standoff here," Anders said. "Katrina's not dead, but she will be if I pull this trigger again. You might shoot me, but I'll still be able to get off a shot. Maybe two."

He was right, Fargo knew. Sometimes even a well-placed bullet wouldn't bring a man down until he had time to fire his weapon.

Possum fell forward onto his face. His guts made a squishing sound on the floor.

"Too bad about Possum," Anders said. "I kinda liked him."

"I didn't," Fargo said.

"Who gives a shit who you liked? Here's what we're gonna do now. I'm going on outside. Half the town will be here in a minute or two, and I'll let them take care of you like they did that sheriff. Possum would've liked that."

Anders backed toward the door.

"You're not going anywhere," Slash said from the boardwalk.

Molly stood beside her. They came inside. Both of them held pistols aimed at Anders' back.

Anders didn't turn when he heard Slash's voice. He kept his pistol trained on Katrina.

"I'll kill the girl, Slash," he said. "You back off."

"From where I'm standing, she looks dead already," Slash said.

"You willing to take the chance?"

"Damn right," Slash said, and she shot him.

Anders didn't shoot Katrina. He started to turn toward Slash, but Molly shot him. Fargo shot him then, and Slash and Molly shot him again. The bullets slapped into him and jerked him from side to side. They kept him upright just long enough for him to pull the trigger of his pistol, but the bullet went into the floor at his feet.

Then the room was quiet again. Smoke floated up toward the ceiling, and the smell of it filled Fargo's nostrils.

Anders crumpled to the floor, not far from Possum.

"I'd've shot him, too," Buck said, " 'cept I figured he was already killed about three times."

Briles was still propped against the door frame. He opened his mouth to speak, but only a croak came out. He cleared his throat and tried again.

"Looks like I win," he said as he slid to the floor.

The crowd that Fargo had been expecting drifted up to the building. Some of the men went over to look at what was left of the destroyed saloon, but most of them wanted to know about Anders.

"He's in there," Fargo said, pointing to the other saloon. "What's left of him."

The more curious went inside to have a look. Most of them didn't seem to care. They wanted to know what would happen to the town.

"It's still here," Fargo said.

"Yeah," said a skinny man with a raw sore on the side of his face. "It's still here, but who's running it?"

Fargo didn't know the answer, but he said, "Briles claims that he is."

"He got carried out of here a minute ago. He's not running anything."

"You'll have to wait and see, then," Fargo said. "Right now, let's say I'm running it."

Nobody seemed to have any objections, so Fargo told the man to go out and cut down Stuver's body.

"Take a couple of men with you and bury him," Fargo continued. "Do it right."

The man seemed about to object, but one look at Fargo changed his mind. He called to three men, and they started down the street.

Fargo watched until they'd gone a good way. Then he said, "The rest of you men go in there and clean the place out. Take Anders and the rest of them off and bury them. Or you can leave them for the wolves for all I care."

"It ain't our job to do that," a man said.

Fargo's hand dropped to his pistol.

"It is now," he said.

There was considerable grumbling, but nobody wanted to test Fargo, not after what he'd done to Anders and his men. After a couple of seconds, people started to move. Fargo left them to it and went over to Slash's place.

Briles was lying on the divan in the parlor with his eyes closed. Slash was sitting beside him. She'd removed his shirt and cleaned up his wound, which was covered with a white bandage.

"He'll live," she said in answer to Fargo's inquiring look. "I'm not so sure that's a good thing. The bullet went clean through his side. Probably nicked a rib, so he'll hurt for a while." She sighed. "I don't know if he was going out there to help you with Anders or to shoot you in the back."

Fargo would have put his money on the second choice. He said, "He still thinks he's going to take over here."

"He might. Nobody else is going to step in. Are you going to send the law in to clean the place up?"

Fargo didn't have any interest in that. Even the citizens of Fort Benton might not care to shut down the town now that Anders was out of the way.

He told all that to Slash, who wondered aloud if Briles was up to the job of running an outlaw town.

"He'll need some help," Fargo said. "Somebody who can take care of him at first and then help him out with the ins and outs of the business end of things. He's not smart enough to do it all himself."

Slash gave him a speculative look. "Who did you have in mind to be this someone?"

"I was thinking of you," Fargo said. "You're smart, you're tough, and you're here. Why not?"

"I hadn't ever thought of it."

Fargo looked at Briles. "Better make up your mind before he gets any better."

"I'll do that," Slash said.

"Good. How's Katrina?"

"She's fine. Just a shoulder wound. I patched her up. The girls are in my room with her. She'll be up and around by afternoon."

That sounded good to Fargo. He was ready to get out of Sundown. He left Slash with Briles and went to look in on Katrina.

He saw her from the doorway. The room was so crowded that he didn't try to go inside. Katrina was sitting up in the bed, and when she saw Fargo, she said, "I want to thank you for what you did."

"You can thank everybody else, too."

"I've done that. I never thought I'd be going home again."

Molly looked at Fargo. "I'd kind of like to go home, too. You think I could go back to Fort Benton with you?"

Fargo said that sounded like a good idea.

"Anders killed Willie," she said. "My husband. He cut off his head."

Fargo told her that he'd heard the story.

"Anders used me, and he whored me out. People might not want me back."

"I don't think anybody'll hold what Anders did against you. Anyway, you took care of him.

"I killed the son of a bitch, all right," Molly said. "Me and Slash. He won't hurt anybody else ever again."

Penny and Lou nodded. Ella said, "I just wish I'd had one good swing at his head with my club."

"Me, too," Molly said. "And after you hit him, I'd still have shot him."

"Would've served the bastard right," Ella said.

Buck was at the livery barn when Fargo caught up with him.

"You like to got Agnes killed," Buck said. "I don't see how she got through the night out there in that street, much less all that shootin' today, and without any feed, besides."

Buck had brought the pinto to the barn, too, and he was seeing to both animals.

"I owe you," Fargo said. "Nobody else in Fort Benton came here to help me."

"They figured they paid you, and that was it," Buck said. "But I kinda thought of you as a friend. A man's gotta help out his friends, same as you helped out Nick,

156

even if he was dead and didn't know what you were doin'."

"I'll help you out, too, if you ever need me," Fargo told him. "Just send me the word."

"I believe you would," Buck said. "By golly, I believe you would."

"You can count on it," Fargo said. "Do you think you can find a buggy or a wagon for Katrina to ride to Fort Benton in?"

"I reckon I can when the owner of this livery comes back. I think he's out helpin' to bury those men we killed."

"Bring it to Slash's place when you're ready," Fargo said.

"Look for me when you see me comin'," Buck said.

Buck showed up in the middle of the afternoon. He was driving a wagon hitched to a couple of mules. Agnes and the pinto were tied to the back of the wagon. Buck reined up in front of the whorehouse and put on the brake. Fargo stood on the porch.

"Well?" Buck asked. "You all set to go?"

"Ready," Fargo said.

Katrina came outside, with Ella holding her good elbow. With Fargo and Ella assisting, Katrina climbed up onto the wagon seat beside Buck.

Slash came out, followed by Penny, Ella, and Lou, as Fargo untied the pinto and mounted up.

"I don't guess we could persuade you to stay a while," Slash said.

Fargo grinned. They'd already talked about that.

"You know I'd like to, but I have to get back to Fort Benton and catch a steamboat."

"You're welcome here any time," Slash said, and the other women nodded.

Molly came out then. She had on a plain cotton dress and carried a little valise.

"You all could come see me in Fort Benton," she said after she hugged each of the women in turn.

They all nodded, but Fargo knew it would never happen. Molly put the valise in the wagon and climbed onto the seat as Katrina moved closer to Buck.

Buck kicked off the brake and snapped the reins. The mules moved forward. Nobody looked back as they left the town.

When they passed between the walls Anders had built, Stuver's body was gone. Fargo wondered how long the people in Fort Benton would remember Stuver. Not for long, he figured.

Then he thought about Marian Cudahy. He had time for at least one more visit before he went back to St. Louis.

He grinned. Maybe more than one.

LOOKING FORWARD!
**The following is the opening
section of the next novel in the exciting
Trailsman series from Signet:**

**THE TRAILSMAN #308
BORDER BRAVADOS**

*Southern Arizona, 1859—if the rattlers and
Apaches don't kill you, then the desperadoes
definitely will.*

The tall, dark rider reined his horse to a sudden halt.
Hand flicking to the Colt .44 on his right hip, he squinted
his lake blue eyes at the cottonwood copse about fifty
yards up the bench on his right.

A large mule deer buck crashed from the serviceberry
and wild currant shrubs at the base of the trees, shook
his head with annoyance, and loped up a cedar-stippled
ridge. Skye Fargo eased his hand away from his Colt's
grips as he watched the thick-necked buck, showing a
gunpowder gray coat and a six-point rack, heavy with
spring velvet, gain the ridge crest and disappear down
the other side.

Fargo snorted, relieved, as he stared at the ridge.
"Don't worry, old-timer. Your meat's too tough for my

palate. I'll wait for something younger and smaller. You have a good summer with plenty of bunchgrass."

Fargo swung around in his saddle, scanning his back trail, one eye squinted against the sun glare. Nothing back there but rocky ridges and cedars, as far as he could tell. But before the buck had startled him, he could have sworn he'd spied a horse-shaped shadow scuttling about that high, granite ridge, quartering southwest.

He'd been over and through that country several times today, and he had nothing to show for his jumpiness but a sense that he was being followed . . .

Shuttling his gaze back and forth across the ridge, he reached for his canteen, popped the cork, and took a pull of the stale water. Beneath him, the Ovaro pinto rippled its withers and blew.

"I know, hoss," Fargo said as he hammered the cork back into the canteen's spout with the heel of his hand, his troubled gaze still quartering over the canyon-split country behind him. "We'll stop soon, and you can have your own drink and a good, long roll." The big, buckskin-clad rider known as the Trailsman took a deep breath and let it out slowly. "Wouldn't mind one of those myself."

Fargo dropped the canteen over the saddle horn and heeled the Ovaro into a walk for several yards, as he continued glancing behind, before urging the magnificent stallion into a trot. A quarter hour later he topped a rise and drew back on the pinto's reins. Below, the five covered wagons of the train he was piloting to a town called Genesis, newly established in Bone Creek Canyon in southern Arizona Territory, lumbered west amidst angling shadows, the dust kicked up by their iron-shod wheels lifting in honey-colored clouds against the copper rocks and boulders on both sides of the trace.

The white canvas covers stretched taut across the ash bows glowed in the soft, westering light. Left of the wagons, a narrow creek meandered against the base of a low sandstone ridge. Above the ridge hung a powder horn moon in the clear desert sky.

Fargo gigged the pinto down the hill. He passed the fifth and fourth wagons. As the pinto moved up to the left front wheel of the third, a voice rose from the driver's box.

"Mr. Fargo!" exclaimed Jasper Felton, a short man with a bib-length, steel-colored beard, a shabby blue bowler on his bald head. He plucked the long yellow foxtail drooping from between his lips. "The missus is growin' mighty wrung out. Can't we stop soon?"

Fargo glanced at the woman sitting beside Felton—a triple-chinned brunette in a poke bonnet whose loose gray dress and multiple aprons could not conceal the fact that she outweighed her husband by a good sixty pounds. Recently a mail-order bride from Ohio, she was pouty and temperamental, though a fair cook.

"I'm about to discuss the matter with Dixon."

Fargo continued on past the next wagon, blinking against the dust churned up by the heavy wheels, and drew even with the first Pittsburgh. The party's leader, Roy Dixon, sat beside his young wife, Deana. Dixon wore his usual bulldog scowl as he leaned forward over his knees, the ribbons of his four-mule hitch in his hands.

He was heading up the party of merchants from Hutchinson, Kansas, to Genesis. Because of its close proximity to planned railroad lines, gold country, and freight trails into Mexico, Genesis was expected to grow as large as Albuquerque in the next ten years.

"Where the hell you been?" Dixon snapped when his eyes found Fargo. "I thought you were supposed to be scoutin' the trail *ahead*. Ain't that why we hired you? Hellfire, with all these blasted washes and Mexican traders' trails out here, we mighta taken a wrong turn and taken the Devil's good time to get back on track!"

Biting his tongue, Fargo pointed ahead, where the creosote-stippled desert rose up against the ridge on the other side of the creek. The ridge flanked the area on three sides, offering protection from all directions but north. "We're gonna stop in that horseshoe of the creek for the night. There's a ford about a mile ahead."

Dixon's goat-whiskered, gray-eyed face blossomed

with anger. "We ain't stoppin' till we get to Genesis! We're almost there, dang blast it!"

Being a religious man—all five wagons were composed of Lutherans who not only intended to establish their own businesses in Genesis, but a Lutheran church, as well—Dixon did not take the Lord's name in vain. That didn't keep him from shooting his mouth off in fine, fire-and-brimstone fashion, however.

Fargo had been humoring the belligerent Bible-thumper for the past three weeks, and he looked forward to unloading the man and his wife, pretty as she was, in Genesis. In fact, he thought he'd probably earned a spot in heaven for not drilling a .44 round through the Lutheran's broad forehead . . . yet.

"Earlier, I thought we could make it today," Fargo said, deftly stitching patience into his voice while staring straight ahead. "But that was before I got a whiff of men on our trail. Besides that, Mrs. Felton's feelin' poorly. We'll stop while we still have enough light to set up camp."

"Hold up there!" Dixon shouted as Fargo pressed his heels to the pinto's flanks. "Time is money, Fargo, and I want to get to Genesis tonight and—" Dixon broke off the tirade, the muscles in his craggy face planing out. "What's that about men on our trail?"

"Last few hours, someone's been foggin' us." He glanced over his shoulder. "I haven't cut any sign, but my sniffer rarely lies . . ."

"What do you suppose they're after, Mr. Fargo?" Mrs. Dixon asked, breathless.

Fargo was happy to have an excuse to shuttle his gaze to the woman. Girl, actually. Fargo didn't think she was a day over twenty. Another mail-order bride, he suspected, though Dixon was tight-lipped about his wife, and, being the proprietary type, kept her bound to her cook pots and water buckets, raising his hackles at any man who gave her more than a passing glance. Fargo had known mules better treated than she.

With gold-blond hair, brown eyes, and delicate features, she was a high-bred filly if he'd ever seen one.

Probably from a wealthy family back east that, having fallen on hard times, had married her off to the pious Kansan.

Fargo tried to keep his eyes from her ample bosom which, he noted in the periphery of his vision, rose and fell sharply, the lightly freckled cleavage opening, the breasts separating, with each inhalation. Her peaches-and-cream cheeks were flushed with worry.

"If they're after anything, it's probably only the mules," Fargo lied.

If whoever was behind them had seen Mrs. Dixon taking her morning ablutions in one of the creeks they'd camped beside, they'd be after more than the mules. Fargo had stumbled upon her once himself and felt as though his heart, gripped by the strong fist of lust, had been turned counterclockwise in his chest.

"Nothin' to worry about, ma'am. Like I said, I haven't cut any sign, so it might only be my imagination. Still, better to hole up before nightfall, though, than to continue in the dark. And, like I said, Mrs. Felton's feelin' poorly."

"You will stay *close*, though, won't you, Mr. Fargo?"

Deana Dixon's eyes were riveted on the Trailsman, one hand spread open on her heaving bosom. Her eyes flicked across the Trailsman's fringed buckskin tunic drawn taut across the iron-hard slabs of his chest.

For a moment, the girl appeared a little faint. Then, her face turning crimson, she looked at her husband, who was scowling at her incredulously. "I mean, he's so well *armed* and all. . . ."

"Don't worry, dear," Dixon growled, clamping his heel down on the two-bore express gun beneath his seat. "I've got old Henrietta here, remember? Not too many men can get past her. Besides"—he canted his head at the girl and winked—"I think Mr. Fargo might be a little trail-addled. I've got keen eyes and ears, too, and I haven't seen or heard anything out of the ordinary."

"That may be true, Dixon," Fargo said, reining his horse in a circle and gesturing for the other wagons to follow him. "But this party will be camping against that ridge this evenin', and that includes your wife. If you want to risk *your* life, that's your business. But I won't let you risk *her* life, as well."

Fargo didn't turn his glance to Dixon's outraged face. Instead, he neck-reined the pinto westward and gigged the horse into an instant, ground-eating lope. A hundred yards ahead, he crossed the creek and scouted the horse-shoe of shoreline rising to the ridge base and carpeted in lush, green grass—mostly grama grass and bluestem, with a sprinkling of tarbrush and catclaw. From the base of the crenellated rock wall behind him, he could see a broad swath of chaparral in three directions.

He sat the pinto, staring at the wagons strung out in a line along the opposite shore. Roy Dixon glared at him from his driver's box, his young wife beside him, both rocking with the wagon's sway. As Dixon approached the ford, he cursed and swung his mules toward the creek.

Fargo smiled and poked his broad-brimmed hat off his forehead. Dixon's team splashed through the water, the wagon following, bouncing sharply as the wheels clattered and barked across the rocks.

The Trailsman waited, watching the other wagons, pleased to see that the second wagon, a heavy-axled freighter driven by the dentist and blacksmith, Merlin Haggelthorpe, didn't ford until Felton's Conestoga was lumbering through the grass toward Fargo. No more than two wagons in a stream at the same time, in case one had trouble and needed assistance.

When all the wagons were safely across, Fargo directed the drivers to line up along the shoreline. Fargo rode up and down the line, giving orders and suggestions. When the wagons were situated and the men were unhitching the teams, Fargo rode back across the creek, and galloped west. He wanted to give the country around them a thorough going-over before dark.

It was Chiricahua country, after all.

Finding little except a herd of mule deer grazing a broad, grassy table two miles northwest, Fargo brought one down with a single shot from his Henry and headed back the way he'd come. It was full dark now, the sky like black velvet upon which a handful of silver dust had been tossed.

Fargo splashed across the creek and turned the horse between two wagons. The pilgrims had built a large cook fire. The men were sitting around drinking coffee and mending harness while the women hauled water from the creek and prepared supper, pots clattering and kindling snapping, the mesquite smoke perfuming the air.

Fargo shoved the field-dressed deer off the back of his horse. It landed with a thud near the fire. The men closed around to look at the fresh meat, their eyes bright with eager anticipation.

They'd run out of fresh game two nights ago, and, since they'd been in Apache country, Fargo hadn't wanted to trigger a shot.

"It's small," he told Mrs. Haggelthorpe, a pale, doughy woman in a burlap dress and apron peeling potatoes near her husband's rickety folding chair. "It should last us till we get to Genesis, though."

"Nice, Mr. Fargo," intoned Jasper Felton, a mule collar draped over his left shoulder, a stout needle in his right hand. "Very nice indeed!"

Fargo began to turn away when he saw a slender figure standing in the shadows off his left stirrup. A pale hand extended a steaming tin cup. "Coffee, Mr. Fargo?"

Deana Dixon's doe-eyed gaze met his. Was she intentionally revealing more cleavage than usual, or was it just his imagination?

Fargo took the cup in his left hand. "Obliged."

"Will you be joining us this evening?" she asked with a wry arch of her brow. "Or is the lone wolf going to tend his own fire again, as usual?"

"I'll be campin' downstream. I can—"

"Yes, I know," said Deana Dixon, her full lips stretching back from her white teeth, brown eyes glinting reflected firelight. "You can see and hear better when you're away from the group."

Fargo found his glance dropping to her bosom, the lace-edged bodice rising and falling slowly, the scalloped lace stretching away from her deep cleavage. It had been a long trip, and he hadn't had a woman in a couple of weeks, but he kept a short leash on his lust.

His own personal rules didn't allow for cavorting with the women in his charge. Sleeping with any woman in a wagon train, least of all a married woman, was akin to hoorawing a herd of bull buffalo with calves.

Fargo raised the cup. "Thanks for the coffee." He pinched his hat brim and glanced toward the fire, his gaze picking out Roy Dixon down on his knees as he and Ben Leonard, an assayer whose wife, Clara, intended to open a haberdashery in Genesis, conferred over the cracked wagon brake Felton held in his hands.

Fargo glanced once more at Deana Dixon on the other side of his horse, smiling obliquely up at him.

He booted the pinto toward the creek.

No other series packs this much heat!

THE TRAILSMAN

**Available wherever books are sold or at
penguin.com**

Penguin Group (USA) Online

What will you be reading tomorrow?

Tom Clancy, Patricia Cornwell, W.E.B. Griffin,
Nora Roberts, William Gibson, Robin Cook,
Brian Jacques, Catherine Coulter, Stephen King,
Dean Koontz, Ken Follett, Clive Cussler,
Eric Jerome Dickey, John Sandford,
Terry McMillan, Sue Monk Kidd, Amy Tan,
John Berendt…

You'll find them all at
penguin.com

Read excerpts and newsletters,
find tour schedules and reading group guides,
and enter contests.

Subscribe to Penguin Group (USA) newsletters
and get an exclusive inside look
at exciting new titles and the authors you love
long before everyone else does.

PENGUIN GROUP (USA)
us.penguingroup.com